I0662733

MY FIRST ONE MILLION YEARS

Frank Aquino

Copyright © 2009 Frank Aquino

All rights reserved.

ISBN: 0980344581
ISBN-13: 978-0-9803445-8-5 (Blencowe Books)

TO IMMUNITY

AGAINST ALL MIND VIRUSES

WHATEVER THE STRAIN

This book is mostly fiction

Then again...what isn't?

CHAPTERS

1

YOU AND ME AND SLICED BREAD

Hi there. My name is Joey. I only found that out quite recently, back in 2000 BC as it turned out, although obviously C hadn't happened by then so calling it BC wouldn't have made much sense. As we'll see, it still doesn't, but that's for later. You'd have to skip to chapter ten to glimpse what I mean by that, but you're not one of those people, are you? This is the story of how I came to be, how I survived all these years, and what brilliant and terrible things I did to your ancestors along the way. I hope you're sitting down.

I'd been nameless for a long time before my naming ceremony (a million years roughly) so I was well and truly ready for a name by the time I got one, but for much of my life I didn't realise how important names were so I didn't complain. Once I got a name however, I was very grateful, otherwise I'd never have been able to do the amazing things I do, and you would never have turned out the way you did.

OK, Joey might not sound like much of a name these days, what with names like Heavenly Hirrani Tiger Lily apparently available, but Joey is what I ended up with and I'm sticking to it.

I think you'll agree that Joey's a pretty simple name but believe it or not the pronunciation is still debated to this day. People who spoke languages before the letter J was invented used to call me Yoey, sometimes Yahweh; occasionally YHWH (yeah, silly I know), and even Yehovah; and some still insist on doing so. But I prefer Joey. I'll tell you why later; first you have to understand me, and that will take a while.

But enough about me for now; let's talk about you. There's no need to introduce yourself; I already know who you are. I've known you for a very long time, and believe it or not you've known me for a lot longer than you realise. That won't make sense to you right now, but it will later on, I guarantee it.

You see I'm very old, old enough to know not just you but also your family, your friends, their friends and pretty much everybody else who is alive today, and who has ever lived. I've been around and I get around. I'm doing all right too – for an orphan. That's right – no parents. If you're moved to sadness, please don't be. It can't be helped. It can't be changed. It's just the way it is. No good crying over it. I don't. In fact even if I had tear ducts, I still couldn't.

But what's really going to knot your rope is that I've never had parents. That's right; never had them. I don't mean I never knew them, I mean I never had them. No mum. No dad. No grannies; nothing. I simply popped into existence one day from absolutely nowhere. I can't tell you the precise date because time hadn't been invented back then, but I know that's exactly what happened. I'll explain what I mean by that in the next chapter, but for the moment let us ponder the strangeness that nobody else knows when they came into existence either.

For eons I've watched people struggle with defining their first memory, the first moment of existence when they stopped being molecular soup and started being alive, and I have to say no one has cracked it yet.

Some people like to think it was the moment they started crying as they flopped out of the womb. Others pretend it was the moment of conception (the Chinese are big on this). Still others believe it was when they first heard their own name spoken, which is a reasonable point I suppose – names being as important as they are; while some very odd people claim to remember waking up inside the womb itself. That's just plain stuff and nonsense of course but personally I like people who believe things like that – they're prime real estate for me; *prime* real estate. You'll understand that odd statement later too, but for now the real truth is that no one really knows when he or she started being alive. At some point they just *know*.

This surprising and uniquely human obsession to *know* is central to my story, and together we will explore it with historical and contemporary examples that might help unscramble the confusion you're feeling right now, but for the time being just hold the thought and enjoy the journey.

Actually if anyone on earth ought to know when they came into existence, it should be me, but for some reason I've never been able to work it out. I suspect it comes down to that name business again. Until people became aware of me and thus conjured me into their minds, I wasn't aware that I existed at all, although I must have existed prior to that point to be able to experience the event so vividly.

Confused? Don't fret – this isn't easy stuff to get your head around. Nevertheless, logic tells me that I must have existed for longer than I know because as soon as I realised I existed, I was already fully competent; I just don't remember being trained. There must have been a training period of some kind, but if there was, the memory completely eludes me. So let's just call it my pre-awareness period and move on to more interesting stuff.

I mentioned already that I've never had parents (which I know you don't believe yet) so what I'm about to say next will really squirt your pistol.

I exist everywhere and I exist nowhere.

Don't close the book! This isn't some mung bean muncher's mystical madness. There's a perfectly rational explanation for what I just said, and I hope to convince you of it if you'll allow me a few more pages.

You see it all makes sense when you realise I'm not a human being. That's right – I'm not like you. In fact I'm not a being at all. I'm an idea. Yes, an idea. A thought. A notion. A concept.

Can you feel me inside your head? Of course you can. I'm in there right now, otherwise why would you be thinking the words *'why would you be thinking the words*?' You didn't create them, I did. I made you think them right here inside your very own head. That's where I live – inside your head.

Don't freak now. I'm not a worm eating your brain. I can't chew through your scull to suck in fresh air or anything alien-like. I'm just an idea, a pattern of chemicals zapping around inside your head. And not just in *your* head, I'm in everyone's head, which is what I meant when I said I exist everywhere.

OK I'm not literally everywhere. I'm not inside the book you're reading, or in the air you're breathing, or in avocados. But I am everywhere inside your own particular world – the world you create for yourself on a daily basis.

Close your eyes for a moment then open them again. Everything went black for a second, but did your world end? You could still feel the book, so the book must have been there. But what about all the things you couldn't feel? Well, if you peeked you'll have verified that everything was still just where you left it (I hope). You see, that world – the world just beyond your eyeballs – is your very own world and no one else's.

Nobody alive today can own this world of yours. Indeed nobody who has ever lived in the past, and nobody who will live in the future can ever experience your particular world. It is yours and yours alone. You made it for yourself, and well done I say. Thanks for letting me in.

The really nice part about creating your own world is that it can never end until you do. You and your world are inextricably linked; which brings me a little closer to my reason for being but not quite there yet. Just hang on a bit longer.

Before you get too smug about world creation, I have to tell you that everyone else has their own world too, which is different to yours – sometimes a little; sometimes a lot; but it's their world and nobody else's. Which means everyone literally does live in a world of their own.

If you've connected the dots by now you'll have figured out that I'm not just in your world, I'm in everyone's. Everyone knows about me, which I why I say I exist everywhere. Just how I got into everyone's world is a fascinating story to be enjoyed later, but for now: trust me, I'm there.

So if I'm everywhere, how can I also be nowhere? Well, as I mentioned earlier I am a thought living inside your mind. Science will tell you that chemicals like sodium and calcium and potassium make your thoughts; but that's not quite right. You see thoughts aren't the chemicals themselves; thoughts are the *patterns* made by the chemicals, in the same way that Morse code isn't the dots; it's the pattern or space between the dots.

Take 'save our souls' for example, shortened to SOS: it goes:

DOTDOTDOT, DOT DOT DOT, DOTDOTDOT. Obviously the dots aren't the message. Dots are just dots. All dots are the same. It's the space between the dots that creates the message.

It's the same thing with thoughts. All thoughts use the same chemicals so it's not the chemicals that make the thought; it's the spaces between them – their shape or pattern if you prefer to think of it that way. Like Morse code, I am the space between the chemicals. I'm in the gaps, the nothingness. *Ergo* I exist nowhere.

Does this make me insignificant; unimportant; a mere curiosity? No! Firmly, no! I am the single most important idea to have ever occurred to the human mind. Since I got my stripes I have totally changed the world and I continue to change it in the most amazing ways that not even I could have predicted.

In my time I have created gods and banished gods; I have raised cathedrals to the sky, and razed cities to the ground. I've made neighbour love neighbour, and neighbour kill neighbour. I have inspired nation building and genocide; treaties and treason, hatred and love, fear and hope. And I've done it all with complete indifference, for I have no emotion at all. Emotion is a human thing, and as I said before, I'm not human. I don't feel; I just do.

So what exactly am I? What kind of thought or idea can make people do all these wonderful and terrible things? Well, it is simply this:

You are going to die one day.

Doesn't sound like much does it? It's not E=MC squared, or sliced bread or anything. It never makes the headlines or gets taught at Harvard or put on fridge magnets or bumper stickers; but believe me it is the single most important idea *ever*.

In the past four billion years since brains of one sort or another have existed, no other kind of mind (and believe me there have been plenty) has ever had this idea except the human kind. After four billion years give or take a million, I popped into someone's head; and once I did, the human race was well and truly screwed. Again I say *well done*.

Speaking of sliced bread, I was there when Otto Rohwedder invented sliced bread, or more precisely the bread slicer. Talk about a guy with no direction in life! Hamlet had nothing on Otto. It was 1912, and Otto was an apprentice jeweller living in the American state of Iowa. He didn't much like being a jeweller so he went to college and did a course in optics – as you do.

I actually don't remember Otto all that well. In fact at the time, I never imagined he would be worth remembering at all. It was only decades later, when sliced bread became the universal benchmark for all human achievement that I realised I should have paid more attention. But I'm pretty sure his ambition in life was to sell jewellery.

So what does he do instead? He invents a machine that slices bread. Go figure. And what a contraption it was. I mean how hard should it have been? Everyone over the age of six already knew how to slice one piece of bread off a loaf using a knife, and although I don't have hands or arms I'd have thought that if you wanted ten slices you'd simply line up nine knives side-by-side, and Robert's your mum's brother.

But oh no; good old Otto arranges sixty pulley wheels at the corners of ten concentric hexagonal rings, arranged rather like a perfect spider web. Then he winds ten flexible saw blades around the pulleys where the webs would have been in the original arachnid version, and drives the whole monstrosity around and around with belts and chains from a huge electric motor.

The extraordinary contrivance comprised two hundred and eight moving parts, covered an entire work bench, and wailed like a sackful of cats. On its inaugural run it cut its one and only loaf into ten slices, caught fire and burnt down the workshop.

I had been inside Otto's head for many years before he made the bread slicer so he already knew he was going to die one day, but as things turned out it wasn't that day. He thus went on to rebuild and perfect his machine, but as we'll see in a moment, it took a while.

In a roundabout sort of way I was the reason he invented his contraption in the first place and did all the other things he did. In fact I'm the reason people do just about everything they do. You see as soon as people realise they are going to die one day they start making plans for cramming in as much as they can before the big day arrives. This is strictly a people thing. Animals are much more laid back; they don't know that they are going to die, even when they're actually dying. Animals live from minute to minute wholly content with the here and now. Lucky for them, they don't even know they are going to get old. The future is something they don't trouble themselves with. They simply can't anticipate a time when they won't feel as good as they feel now. In short, they don't make plans for old age and death the way people do.

What about squirrels, I hear you say? Squirrels hoard nuts for the winter – *ergo* they plan for winter, right?

Wrong, but thanks for getting this far. As it happens I know quite a bit about squirrels from personal experience. How? Not so long ago (well, relatively anyway – it was in the 12th Century) I tried to get inside a squirrel's head by convincing a rather grubby little Italian chap from Umbria, (Assisi I recall) whose name was Giovanni di Bernardone, to tell a squirrel that it was going to die one day, and that it should make preparations for entering the great nut-bar in the sky.

You know Giovanni quite well, but this name won't ring any bells just yet. His mum named him Giovanni in honour of *San Giovanni Battiste* (or Saint John the Baptist if you prefer) because she expected her handsome lad to be a great religious leader – religion being one of the more lucrative businesses of the time. And Giovanni thought this was a pretty good idea; but his dad surely didn't.

Dad's communication with his wife was about as good as any husband's before or since, so Mrs Bernardone knew nothing about what Mr Bernardone was planning. Mr Bernardone had already made plans inside his head that young Giovanni would take over the family business importing goods from France then selling them to the local Umbrians and Romans at exorbitant prices. It was a perfectly honourable profession destined to keep the Bernardone family in clover for years to come – or so he thought.

The trouble was he neglected to mention this fantasy to his wife. Moreover, when he told his son Giovanni about how life was going to unfold for him, and that he should get used to the idea of being a shopkeeper for the next fifty years, Giovanni instantly revised his opinion of his father's sanity, and told him shove it.

But dad was clearly away with the fairies, seeing Giovanni's rebellion as a mere minor setback. Somehow he concluded that if he changed Giovanni's name to Francesco in honour of France's commercial splendour, then the boy would magically absorb his father's clarity of mind, and miraculously change his. Funny how some humans can add two and two together and get marshmallow; but lucky for me they do.

Not only did the newly and forcibly baptised Francesco continue to angrily oppose his father's map of the future, he got so screwed-up by his parents' incessant quarrelling that he rebelled against both of them and chose the worst of both worlds. He denounced his father's love of all things commercial, and instead began a fundamentalist religious cult that his mother utterly abhorred, and which earned him nothing if you exclude a posthumous sainthood, which didn't help pay the bills while he was alive.

Francis (his more familiar name in case you haven't twigged yet) already had a thing for the animals of Assisi. In fact he loved animals so much that one of the founding principles of his religious cult was to never wash his body lest harm came to the creatures that lived on it. This alone destined him for a life of isolation, irrespective of his other odd practices.

So he and his anosmic followers spent quite a bit of time in the bush. Theirs was a lonely existence, and with so few conversation partners around, it wasn't a big stretch for me to get Francis chatting to squirrels instead.

There were hoards of red squirrels in the Italian countryside back then, so finding a squirrel around Assisi was as easy as finding a rat in Venice. Nowadays the countryside is all *autostrade* and pizza boxes and olive pips, but back then the place was largely untouched. Animals got a halfway decent shot at life before the blunderbuss was invented, and people started taking full-way decent shots at them.

Anyway, Francis did his best, speaking softly and surprisingly eloquently for someone with just a squirrel for an audience, but he couldn't push me into the squirrel's brain. In fact I didn't get much past the squirrel's ears, but for the brief moment I was there I got a glimpse of squirrel-world, and believe me, while they're awake, squirrels have only one thing on their mind: collecting. They aren't like you. They have no sense of future. They are simply wired up to collect stuff. They collect acorns because they like acorns, but when there are no acorns around, they don't stop collecting; they simply collect whatever happens to be edible.

So, what if there's nothing edible lying around, I hear you ask? Well they just keep on collecting whatever they can lay their cute little mitts on, which, by the way, is why they'll pinch your car keys if you leave them lying on the grass. Squirrels aren't saving for winter; they're just collecting. When it's too cold to go outside, their desire to stay warm overrides their urge to collect, so they quite sensibly stay indoors and eat the pile acorns that happens to be in there with them. Future doesn't come into it.

If squirrels really did have a sense of future, they wouldn't just collect acorns, they'd organise themselves into gathering teams, storage teams, distribution teams and waste disposal teams. They'd have acorn brokers and an Acorn Stock Exchange and run acorn hedge funds (maybe even grow acorn hedges) which would be a far more effective way to plan for the winter.

But squirrels aren't planners, they're collectors, compelled by the same forces that compel men to fart and women to shop: instinct, not insight.

Moreover, in every animal mind that I've ever tried to penetrate, I've hit the same brick wall. They just can't conceptualise beyond the here and now. Only humans can do that. Humans are therefore my playground.

So, just to finish off the story of Otto and the bread slicer; Otto invented his first bread slicer in 1912 and perfected it in 1928. This is not a typo; it really did take him sixteen years to get his mechanical marvel working well enough for someone to buy it, at which point an ad man coined the utterly uninspiring advertising slogan (and I quote):

The greatest forward step in the baking industry since bread was wrapped.

I have to say that people's comparison skills back then were as dull as something really, really dull.

As I mentioned before, Otto knew he would get old and die one day, just like everyone else, so his plan was to be rich before that happened, which is why he invented the bread slicer. As things turned out it didn't make him rich (nothing did) but that's the way it goes. Nevertheless he invented it because of me.

The point of my telling you Otto's story wasn't so much to brag, but to say something about ideas. Ideas can come in a flash, but they can take a very long time to evolve into something special. Take me for example. I took about ten seconds to pop into existence, but I took almost a million years to get good at what I do. And believe me I have gotten very, very good at what I do.

He-he; here is how it all started.

2

MOMMY MUKTUK AND THE GIANT LEAP

I was born in Chad, Africa. I think I can say *born* can't I? *Born* isn't reserved for the exclusive use of sexual reproducers is it? Ideas can be born without having to fight their way out from between some gal's legs. Stars can be born without a whole lot of afterbirth messing up the sky. So I'm going to claim I was born. In Chad.

Of course Chad wasn't called Chad back then because the idea that land might need a name hadn't occurred to anyone yet. Animals and people and trees and berries and water and storms and lightning and penises all had names, but not the land. When the hairy hominids of the day wanted to express the concept of land they just spread their arms wide and gazed at the horizon, which was pretty boring conversation, even for a specie with just ninety words in its vocabulary, excluding grunts and screams.

I mention screams here as a segue to my birth, because it was almost certainly a scream that triggered Muktuk to give birth to me. Muktuk is the gal I have come to regard as my mom, even though I can't really prove she is. Here is what I mean.

Chad was a lush place back then (I'm talking a million years now) and by and large the hairy folks that lived there ate pretty well. But there were occasional droughts, and my birth year happened to be one of them. The rains were very late, and even though Muktuk's group could still find food, it took quite a bit more effort to get a decent feed.

One day, Muktuk couldn't find enough insects and berries on the branch she was occupying, so she started edging along the branch to jump to another tree where she'd noticed bees flying back and forth. Back then everyone agreed that honey was worth risking stings for, and even worth making dangerous jumps for, but as it turned out, this particular jump would be far more dangerous than she could ever have imagined, if she'd had imagination, that is.

Meanwhile a little further up the branch, a big lunk called Raak, who used to rape Muktuk annoyingly often, had just pumped the contents of his testicles into his auntie Lukluk, and was as a consequence feeling even more dim-witted than usual.

Post-coital male idiocy had played a major role in shaping the world up to this point (I was later to learn it always would) and once I started paying attention to such things, it became apparent to me that more than just sperm gets ejected during the male orgasm. A heavy dose of common sense goes along for the ride, creating a sexually imposed brain drain that over the eons has been responsible for some seriously bad decisions, including the one I'm about to describe.

Raak knew that Muktuk was the smartest gal in the clan because she had the best eyesight and the best colour vision – both handy for spotting ripe fruit in the mostly green canopy. She also had the best memory of where to find the best food, so Raak liked to stick close by her at feeding time, which was pretty much whenever he wasn't stalking other females. When he saw her edging along the branch, and then spied the beehive, he figured out what she was up to and acted without a second thought; or a first one really.

Salivating like a rabid hyena he bounded past her and launched himself into the ten-foot gap between the trees, in a typically selfish attempt to get to the honey first. Five feet into the jump he spotted the leopard waiting by the beehive, and spent the final five feet screaming in anticipation of what was coming next. His screaming actually stopped once the leopard clamped its jaws around his throat; but it was hard to tell because by then everyone else was screaming too.

It was a scary moment in the lives of these simple folk, and everyone fled the tree in panic – everyone that is except Muktuk.

Muktuk was different. She ate better food than the others, so her brain had been growing bigger than the others'. Being just nine years old, she still had a smallish skull, which meant her brain had to compress and fold over itself to fit inside her little cranial box. This folding process, which is still evident in brains today, forced millions of new brain cells to meet and exchange information, giving her new insights into what was happening around her. It also gave her quite a bit more memory compared to everyone else; and headaches too – an affliction that is still evident in women today, particularly at mating time.

When Muktuk saw Raak being eaten by the leopard, her brain was of course flooded with fear chemicals that made her scream and shake like everyone else. Fear chemicals had been around forever, and had become the head-honcho chemicals of the brain. They took priority in all unpleasant situations, and generally hijacked all decision-making. But this time Muktuk got a dose of something else as well – chemicals that she usually only got when she discovered something new that might be edible, namely curiosity chemicals. She'd grown to love the sensation of curiosity because it was usually followed by a hit of pleasure whenever she satisfied it, so she decided to wait and see if it would happen again.

By now Raak resembled a Picasso painting, but despite her urge to flee the horrific scene, Muktuk kept watching and she reached a landmark conclusion that would affect the future of all humankind. She admitted to herself that she hadn't seen the leopard either. She'd been planning to do exactly what Raak had done, and, save for a bit of luck, she'd be dead by now instead of Raak. What then followed was the most original thought in human history so far.

She thought: *I am going to die one day.*

And suddenly I popped into existence.

Thanks mom. I love you, but I wish you'd given me a name.

3

YOU'RE GOING TO DIE ONE DAY

Mommy Muktuk, I came to realize as the years went by, was a real blabbermouth. Addicted to curiosity and the pleasure that came from satisfying it, she started experimenting with everything she saw just to get a hit. Her swollen brain began inventing words by the hundreds to describe the new things she was learning each day. She quickly worked out that if she was going to die one day, then so was everyone else. Mostly she didn't care about them, but she found she had an uncontrollable urge to pass this vital information on to her kids. And she had plenty.

By the grand old age of fifteen Muktuk had been impregnated six times by six different males, all lumbering oafs with exactly two life-goals, namely eat as much as possible and rape as much as possible (these guys weren't called *Homo Erectus* for nothing). I learned a lot about males at this time because as Muktuk developed language she passed me into her offspring, two of which were boys. As the boys developed into adulthood, they gave me a first-hand squint through the pinhole camera that is the male mind, and believe me, food and sex pretty well covered it. Sport didn't come along till much later.

Unburdened by loftier ambitions males were expert in their two *raisons d'etre,* namely gulping huge chunks of food without chewing properly, and squirting sperm into the nearest cervix with hypodermic precision. With their minds and bodies thus fully occupied, males had little interest in the concept of look-before-you-leap, so by Muktuk's sixteenth year only one of her mates had lived long enough to wonder why his so-called kids didn't all look and smell like he did. Fortunately he didn't have the brain capacity to frame a decent question around it, so the issue was never seriously raised. And besides, he was too distracted by his main interests to hold the thought for very long anyway,

So, thanks to the rampant infidelity in the clan, Muktuk ended up with quite a diverse spread of DNA to play with, and I must say she produced some very weird looking sprogs as a result; but whatever was causing her brain to grow bigger, it was all her own doing and none of her mates', because all her kids inherited big brains regardless of who daddy was. Consequently when she taught her kids language including the unpleasant revelation that they were going to die one day, they all understood it perfectly clearly. Or to put it another way, they understood *me*.

What eventually killed mommy Muktuk, incidentally, was her tendency to make babies with big brains. Big brains of course meant big heads, but unfortunately her cervix was never kept in the loop, and such miscommunication was always going to end badly. Eventually a kid with a bowling ball of a head got stuck at the wrong end of her birth canal and never saw the light of day. So that was that for Muktuk and for any ambitions that big brains might have had for growing even bigger, at least until other parts of female anatomy caught up. But at least she died knowing she was right: she really was going to die one day.

The chain reaction that Muktuk started back then has dispersed me widely throughout the human collective, and is still going strongly. I have grown a lot since then, and now I exist in several forms I'll discuss later, but for nine hundred thousand years I stayed more or less the same as when Muktuk had me. I saw no reason to change. Reminding people that they were going to die one day was a pretty cushy job, and I was quite prepared to just sit inside their heads and enjoy the ride, prodding them with the bad news from time to time.

Now before you condemn me as a slack bludger lacking ambition, I should mention in my defence that competition in the cranium was pretty fierce. I wasn't the kingpin of the old grey matter club – not by a long shot. Despite having kick-started a new line of thinking, and having galvanized the pre-human race into paying a tad more attention to the business of staying alive, I was still a relative minion. I never imagined getting get a seat at the big-boys' table, so I wasn't disposed to making trouble.

In brains back then, and even today, two other chemical patterns hogged the limelight. These were *fear,* whom I've already mentioned; and another one you'll recognize immediately called *the pleasure of believing you're right,* but is usually shortened to *self-esteem* (or *arrogance* if it has put itself in charge).

One or the other of these two guys pretty well ran the whole show. I wasn't in their league, so they completely ignored me. It took me eons to figure out how to get onside with them, but let me tell you, when I did, I got handed the most fantastic, jaw-dropping, awe-inspiring, career-building opportunity of a lifetime.

What created that opportunity was, coincidentally, also about food. But this time it wasn't about a scarcity of food; it was about abundance. Here's what happened.

4

SHARMAH'S MAMMOTH TRAP – AND YOURS

About a hundred thousand years ago my hosts no longer resembled the hairy *Homos* that Muktuk had been dropping like ripe guava nine hundred thousand years prior. In fact they looked quite a bit like you, only not as fat. Food was still the preoccupation it always had been, but these guys had developed a special taste for meat. Trouble was, meat came from other animals not keen on parting with it, so *Homo Neanderthalensis* and *Homo Sapiens* (my two latest surviving models) had to work hard to get it. There were plenty of berries and leaves and roots lying around to be picked and eaten, but such titbits were well down the bottom of the menu near the children's meals. My guys didn't want carrots and nuts, they wanted meat, in fact they were hooked on it; and the biggest lump of meat around back then was the woolly mammoth.

Bringing a mammoth down was hard and dangerous work. It took a lot of spears and a lot of casualties, but it was worth it for whoever survived the ordeal. Yet as hard as it was to kill a mammoth, the real challenge was keeping up with one. These were migratory animals with very long legs and big lungs – the original fast food – and if you wanted mammoth burger, you had to chase after one for nine or ten miles and hope it got a stitch before you did. Otherwise, forget it; it wasn't worth it anymore – just eat more nuts and berries, and pretend you chose vegetarianism for noble reasons. But if you could bring a mammoth down, you and the tribe ate well. Very well.

Muktuk's big-brained descendents were now full of ideas. It's amazing how inventive they'd become once they realized they could put off the inevitable by using their brains for more than just keeping their ears apart. And they invented some amazing stuff, almost all of it for killing something. But the one thing they invented that interested me most was imagination. I'd watched imagination grow for thousands of years, and I sensed it had the potential to turn me into something really special, but since I didn't have it myself, I just couldn't imagine how.

By this age, which would one day be called the Stone Age, people were using their newfound imagination in spectacular ways. For example, instead of just chasing a mammoth till it dropped from exhaustion, some of them imagined a future in which a mammoth might fall down a ravine and break its legs, thus slowing it down long enough to get its belly sliced open with a sharp flint axe. Yum. Then one day rather than just imagine it, one guy called Sharmah realized he could make it happen.

Sharmah was a lazy bastard at the best of times: skinny as a reed and smelled of wild onions and dung. But he had a surprisingly good brain despite the poor nourishment he gave it. That's another thing I've noticed over the years: the least deserving individuals often get the best deal. Random chance accounts for a lot more than you might think. For example, unpleasant as Sharmah was, he had the gift of the gab and a voice that sounded nice and carried far upwind, which was where everyone seemed to be whenever he was around.

Without telling the chief what he was up to, Sharmah convinced the more gullible in the tribe to form into two mobs. He told one mob to hide in the trees near a well-worn mammoth track that ran close to a cliff edge, and the other to wait at the foot of the cliff with spears and axes at the ready.

Sure enough a young mammoth came lumbering down the track looking forward to a long and happy life when, as instructed, Mob A came screaming out of the trees frightening the poor creature half to death. The sight of so many crazed people panicked the creature into a blind run and it plummeted down the cliff to Mob B where it got sliced and diced until it was dead meat. What's more, nobody else died in the hunt, which was very unusual.

Sharmah-the-stinky's idea had worked an absolute treat, and it instantly skyrocketed him from a nobody to a superstar. Dung and onions was suddenly musk of the day.

I was inside Sharmah's head (and everyone else's for that matter) when the chief forgave him for arranging unauthorised projects behind his back, and he even presented him with the choicest cut of meat as a reward.

The flood of pleasure chemicals that bathed Sharmah's brain was an absolute sight to see. I mean a sight to see. His level of ecstasy surpassed even the time he'd snuck up behind his slow-witted cousin Buglana and slipped her one. Yes, this latest tsunami of pleasure was far bigger and lasted far longer than sex ever could.

I watched pleasure flood Sharmah's brain for hours while he milked the limelight for all it was worth; and I got firsthand experience of how much people love being right. The lazy prick had had one good idea in his awkward seventeen years of life, and now the tribe considered him a genius. They loved him; and why not? After all, he'd given them a guaranteed meat supply forever, apparently. You'd have to love that, wouldn't you? Sharmah never felt so good; he wanted it to go on and on and on.

This was the pivotal point in his life (and yours too, by the way, but I'll get to that later) because his new celebrity status meant that from then on, pretty much everything he said and did was also right – whether it actually was or not.

The chemical co-mingling in his brain lasted so long that something special happened to me too. My own chemicals got mixed up with the pleasure chemicals saturating his skull, and we all kind of stuck together. After that, every time I reminded Sharmah that he was going to die one day, he felt pleasure. I don't mean he felt pleasure about dying, I mean he felt pleasure about knowing he was right about it.

Believing they were right, it seemed, was more important to humans than what they were right about, or indeed whether they were actually right or not. The key element was the pleasure, not the validity. This I found interesting.

Sharmah started experimenting with his newfound pleasure-source by making up stories just to see if people would believe him, and thus deliver a fresh hit. His stories were harmless enough at first. For example he would wisely proclaim that mammoths were more easily spooked at midday because they couldn't see their shadows; and only certain kinds of screams frightened certain kinds of mammoths – high-pitched screams frightened female mammoths, low pitched growls frightened male mammoths. It was all nonsense but his audience lapped it up because he was so wise. His pleasure grew more intense; and more needed.

Then self-interest took over. Entrepreneur that he was, he started making up lies that would not only benefit him mentally; he started telling lies that benefited him materially. His prize creation was to insist that he was obviously too important to the tribe to risk his life hunting. He should really stay back at the cave where it was safe, and where his ideas and creativity could flow freely. All the women stayed in the cave during hunting trips too, but that was mere coincidence he argued. His safety and comfort were essential to the good of the tribe. But he would still need the best cut of meat to feed his ideas, of course.

With bellies packed full of mammoth meat, and with an apparently guaranteed and continuous meat supply on hand, it was easy for everyone to agree with him.

Sharmah was now Sharmah-the-wise. He had achieved superstar status with just one good idea, and achieved near chieftain-like status by lying through his teeth. His self-esteem soared, and ever after it was inextricably linked to how much he could make people admire him.

This was the first time I'd twigged that self-esteem was actually the sole driving force of human behaviour. Up until then I assumed that the environment played the deciding role, which seemed to explain why behaviour appeared so random. But once I started paying attention to such things I realised everything humans did (yes, everything) had its roots in the simple question: *how will this affect my self-esteem?* Any proposed actions that might boost people's opinions of themselves were perfectly OK to execute irrespective of the consequences; whereas any proposed actions that might threaten that self-view was not OK – also irrespective of the consequences. The key component was the effect on self-esteem. What a simple and effective test it is? But oddly it's quite awkward to explain.

If you're a human being, you might choose to be offended by what follows but please let me explain. It took me a long time to work out what self-esteem was, because despite the smug feeling of superiority that it apparently invoked in people, they didn't seem to know precisely what caused it. I had to work it out for myself by observation.

It turns out that self-esteem is actually the future tense of survival. Survival is, obviously, a past tense thing. Survival is a statement that you just survived the most recent threat; that you're still here to enjoy the feeling of having survived. Self-esteem, on the other hand is about believing that your current survival means you obviously have the right stuff to survive the next threat – that you've got life all figured out; that you've got the right tools for the job, and you're pretty well untouchable. Incidentally I don't wish to belittle self-esteem – it's an essential survival skill. Without it you'd be too terrified to venture out of the cave, convinced that you probably wouldn't make it through the day. But sorting out what contributes to survival and what simply tags along to make you feel smug, must surely be more important than simply revelling in the smugness itself.

Even today I can see that humans believe maintaining and boosting self-esteem is the most important thing they can do to extend life, but they are surprisingly sloppy about differentiating what causes it. Self-esteem itself becomes the reason they've survived rather than the specific knowledge or skill that they employed to achieve current survival. They take a blunt-instrument approach to what is a very intricate problem. Every moment that they've survived reinforces the notion that all their currently held beliefs, behaviours, skills and knowledge are what got them through the day safely, and will continue to do so. Often that's right; often that's wrong, but without unbiased self-critical analysis they'll never know what actually works, and what just tags along for the ride.

Unfortunately sorting the wheat from the chaff in this endeavour requires self criticism and is thus unpleasant to do, so after a while it becomes easier not to try. With self-esteem firmly rooted in everything they currently believe – whether it makes sense or not – they dare not tinker with perfection because they have survived perfectly well up to now. Why question a good thing?

This for example is why some children will never step on a crack in the pavement – because they never have in the past and they've always survived – so crack-avoidance becomes an essential act for survival. It is also why thieves might continue stealing well beyond the point of accumulating adequate wealth; or why sportsmen might continue to compete until they break a bone, or even die; or why believers in the supernatural dare not question their beliefs.

It was also the reason why Sharmah chose never to wash his body ever again after he invented the mammoth trap – just in case his repellent odour had something to do with his self-perceived brilliance; so he continued that notion into everything he did. For example knowing which foods were edible and which were poisonous based on past experimentation was a useful skill for anyone in Sharma's day. Such ability could boost self-esteem considerably when showing others what to eat and what to avoid. But believing his brilliance somehow originated from his body odour ran a serious risk of killing him next time an unfamiliar mushroom was tasted.

But as I mentioned already, Sharmah was the luckiest bastard on Earth. He played this kind of dangerous game, and amazingly he got away with it for a surprisingly long time. I'll tell you how he died, at the end of my story. It happened while he was eating, but it wasn't due to eating mushrooms; it was due to his self-esteem.

So unanalysed, self-esteem can lead to some pretty distorted conclusions and behavious. Worse still, the consequences (good or bad) of such confused beliefs often occur days, weeks or even years after the belief has taken root, so the consequence is rarely linked to the cause.

So, back to Sharmah. Inventing the mammoth trap was good for Sharmah's self-esteem, and lying through his teeth had boosted it to such unprecedented heights that he decided it was lying that caused it. So he figured more was better.

For several months thereafter, everything was hunky-dory. Fresh meat kept coming through the cave door, his self-esteem burgeoned, and he grew even lazier. Then something worrying happened. Tribesmen began reverse-engineering his mammoth trap, adapting it to trap other animals, and pretty soon everyone was claiming credit for this idea or that. This endangered Sharmah's status as the tribe's one and only ideas-man. It started to dawn on even the most dim-witted members of the tribe that good ideas might not be the sole domain of Sharmah-the-charmer.

As the first celebrity on earth, Sharmah milked the upside for as long as he could, but he soon learned that the downside of being in show business was having to perform regularly and well. If he didn't keep the ideas coming, he'd start smelling like dungy onions again. In other words, to preserve his god-like status (that is, his self-esteem), he would have to come up with something special.

I mentioned god deliberately here because god wasn't a word anyone had used yet. Sure, the lightning and rain and thunder and volcanoes and blizzards and diseases that tormented the tribe were feared and revered, and were given special names worthy of awe and wonder, but they weren't endowed with supernatural powers. They couldn't be; they were simply the powers of nature. They were what they were.

No one had yet thought to bestow nature's power onto abstract forms and call them gods. It wasn't because they were trying to preserve the purity of nature; it was simply that they didn't have time to ponder such esoteric concepts. As I said, until Sharmah came along, everyone had been fully occupied finding food and keeping warm and avoiding animal teeth.

Then along comes Sharmah with all this free time on his hands and changes all that. As it turned out he had a lot more free time on his hands than even he expected because he was getting a whole lot less sex than he imagined a superstar should get. This was largely his own doing. Success hadn't improved his smell one bit, and after nine hundred thousand years, women had become a lot more picky about whom they bent over for.

So our stinky friend literally had more free time on his hands than anyone I'd ever occupied up to that point in time, and with all that time to sit and think, I expected him to come up with something really special. Fire had been tamed already; drawing on cave walls never occurred to him; and iPods were a touch beyond him. Finding something better than his unpatented mammoth trap wasn't going to be as easy as he thought.

After six months of bludging, he came up with zilch. Nothing. *Niente*. Nout. His celebrity status was nearing rock bottom. He had very few fans left, and things weren't looking hopeful at all. Even the chief was spending more time upwind. Worse still the mammoths had learned to avoid the tribe's clumsy ambushes, so the meat supply was starting to dwindle. Eventually Sharmah found it politically wise to stay out of sight by moving into a cave of his own a mile or so from the main cave.

Then came a breakthrough. One late afternoon he was making his way to the main cave to find out why his steaks hadn't turned up, when just as he got within sight of the tribe he noticed a stick lying in the mud. It was about the right length for a walking stick or handy short spear so he picked it up. As he did so, the stick left a curvy impression in the mud, which, in the dimming light with leaf shadows playing over it, looked for all the world like a snake was under it. Being scared to death of snakes he let out a blood-curdling scream that brought the tribe running.

When the first runner got to Sharmah he found him convulsing on the ground and frothing at the mouth. Luckily, Sharmah had flung the stick away as he fell. Why lucky? Well, one observation I have made in my million-year study of humans is that the fastest runners are often the slowest thinkers. The runner saw the same snake-like impression in the mud and concluded that Sharmah had been bitten by the snake that made it. Clearly the great man was dying from snakebite.

I was inside the sprinter's head of course and reminded him that everyone dies one day, and not to worry about it. He felt pretty good about remembering that, and he transferred the good feeling of being right onto his mistaken conclusion about the snake, declaring himself to be correct about that too.

By the time the second runner arrived, the first runner reinforced his joy of being right by telling the new arrival that he'd just missed seeing the snake slither away. From then on there were two eyewitnesses to the non-existent snake.

Sharmah's contortions, incidentally, were due to what today would be called a grand mal seizure. This sudden onset of epilepsy at age seventeen cleared up a couple of things that had been troubling me for some time about Sharmah, namely why he was so smart, and why he smelled so bad. I went poking around inside his head and saw that he had several brain cysts. One cyst was stimulating his parietal lobe, which explained his ability to imagine things others could not. A second cyst was in his still-primitive frontal lobe that was supposed to control social skills, so that was no surprise. But a third cyst was smack in the middle of his olfactory cortex, and was gumming up a lot of brain wiring.

I can say now with confidence that if Sharmah had lived to age forty five (which he didn't – such an age was still unheard-of) he would have been the first human on Earth to get Alzheimer's disease, an early precursor of which is a deteriorating sense of smell. But the Stone Age was a dangerous place; Sharmah would die well before then.

Eventually the whole tribe arrived and gathered around Sharmah's shaking body, including the chief whom by now had had a gut-full of Sharmah's antics. But Sharmah was nothing if not the luckiest bastard on earth. Instead of swallowing his tongue and dying like any self-respecting epileptic back then, he only half-swallowed it, making it clear to one and all that he was choking on something round and slimy.

As the crowd gathered around and did more talking than listening (an affliction that has escalated to pandemic levels in modern times) the snake story mingled with the swallowing story, grew legs and began to run through the crowd like wildfire, convincing one and all that the great Sharmah had swallowed a live snake. Clearly the snake was trying to escape, making Sharmah writhe and squirm, but Sharmah wouldn't let it escape.

The seizure lasted long enough for the new snake-swallowing story to reach a deafening volume, drowning out rival stories and thus making it true, whereupon Sharmah stopped writhing and went stiffer than a mammoth's tusk.

Everyone suddenly shut-up.

It was now quiet enough for the two runners who'd been trying to tell everyone that the snake had slithered away, to quietly admit they might have been mistaken. In hindsight they agreed it now seemed much more likely that Sharmah had swallowed the snake. Everyone cheered at their conversion, and the runners felt like they were part of the tribe again.

Never once did anyone think to question whether or not there had been a snake at all. Why spoil a good story with a bunch of impertinent questions, I say. Everyone felt much better believing the same thing that everybody else believed. Asking awkward questions was just going to annoy people whom you might have to rely upon later. This is another aspect of humanity that has helped me along my path to greatness: brazen fiction beats boring fact every time.

Suddenly, to everyone's shock, Sharmah's muscle rigidity softened and he stopped breathing entirely. I reminded the onlookers once again that everybody dies one day, but this time they rebelled against me, united in their belief that Sharmah would be the exception. Obviously Sharmah was more powerful than a mere snake. He would absorb the snake's power and venom, and thus make the tribe invincible. Everyone knew it.

After a minute or so, the chief poked Sharmah sharply in the ribs with his spear. At the time, I was distracted by the riot going on inside everyone's head so I'm not entirely sure the chief wasn't just poking Sharmah for the sheer joy of it, but true to form Sharmah-the-charmer flinched and woke up to the cheers and jubilation of his worshipers. The chief got special praise too, since he had obviously revived the great man with the prod. Sharmah was back, and even the chief felt strangely comforted by his familiar stench.

The triumphant crowd picked up Sharmah and carried their hero back to the main cave where they gave him pride of place by the fire, begging to hear what had happened.

Sharmah began speaking, and after a few words it was obvious (to me only) that whatever had temporarily seized his brain, certainly hadn't affected his bullshit circuits. He entertained the crowd for hours with stories drawn not just from his active imagination but also from the vivid hallucinations he'd experienced during the seizure.

Sharmah was so convinced the hallucinations had really happened, he invented new words and concepts to describe them, like *near death experience* and *other-world* and *back from the dead* and *afterlife*, and my personal favourite: *spiritual*. The tribe loved *spiritual* the most; even though none of them including Sharmah himself had the foggiest idea what it meant. It just sounded good. Moreover Sharmah felt positively magical when everyone craned their necks and waited for him to explain it. But puppet master that he was, he kept them dangling, closing his eyes wisely and slowly shaking his head, making it clear to one and all that *spiritual* was a special word for him and him alone. The crowd lapped it up. His self-esteem almost exploded.

I, as you might imagine, was mightily pissed off. For almost a million years I'd been telling everyone they were going to die one day; that it was a bad thing; and more recently I'd been giving them a hit of pleasure whenever they remembered it. Then out of leftfield, Sharmah hands them eye-witness proof that death was not going to be so bad after all – that there was something on the other side to look forward to. He'd been there; how could anyone, including me, possibly refute it? Moreover he'd come back with a detailed report! This looked serious. My days were numbered, I was sure of it. But oh, how wrong I was.

Sharmah eventually ran out of stories, and succumbed to fatigue brought on by his fit. Ever the showman, and aware of his special status, he made a grand exit by choosing a warm and willing groupie from his burgeoning fan club. Then he led her to a secluded inner cave for some smelly slap and tickle.

The tribe however, was still pumped up by the day's events and weren't ready for bed just yet. Instead, the young men started showing off their hunting prowess for the ladies, using their recent caribou kill as subject matter.

With mammoth temporarily off the menu the men had been forced to hunt caribou – a beast less favoured because of its sharp senses, sharp antlers and sharply nasty disposition. Usually it was hard to even get close to one. But using a modified version of Sharmah's hide-and-surprise method for hunting mammoth, the men had divided into four teams to encircle a small herd for an all-sides attack. In the mayhem two spears from opposite teams found their marks in a single caribou, bringing the beast down.

All through the butchering process and later during dinner, a friendly argument bounced back and forth about which team had inflicted the fatal wound. With Sharmah's heavy entertainment over, the men craved something lighter, so they devised a means by which the women could decide which team killed the beast.

Using the caribou's unpalatable bladder inflated with air to represent the entire animal, a few elected members of each team re-enacted the hunt using not their spears, which would have put a premature end to the fun, but using their feet instead. The lads had so much fun kicking the bladder around that they played well into the night, well past the point when the women had stopped caring and had gone to bed, marking the beginning of a long and enduring tradition that still survives in suburban lounge rooms today. Indeed if it hadn't been for the fire's going out for lack of tending, the lads would surely have played till dawn.

I didn't realise it at the time, but the lads had invented a following that would one day come to rival my own. But for the next fifty thousand years, until an enormous glut of home-delivered food would change everything, football would remain nothing more than a hunters' ritual for deciding who killed what.

The lads finally went to sleep, blissfully ignorant of the staggering events that would unfold the following day, which would change their lives forever; and yours.

5

THE AFTERLIFE AND OTHER TRICKS

Next morning, everyone was feeling invincible just like Sharmah, and decided to go mammoth hunting like in the good old days. Personally I thought it was a bad idea because they'd been playing footy into the wee smalls and were dog-tired despite their youthful enthusiasm. Sharmah was still fast asleep and had no idea what was going on; and whether or not he'd have tried to discourage them is something I've pondered over the eons, but as it turned out, tiredness played right into his hands (and mine too, if I'd had any).

Since the local mammoths had found another route to the river, which didn't include a nearby cliff, the tribe had to revert to the old way of chasing them down. By around lunchtime, after a four-hour run, three of the fittest hunters had come close to having the world's first heart attacks, but had also managed to wear down an old male by spearing it six times in its back legs. The beast eventually went down; or rather sat down like a domestic dog might in a defensive position with its back against a rock, not ready to give up the ghost just yet. Then one of the hunters, himself barely able to stand from exhaustion went in for the kill and got gored to death for his trouble.

While the mammoth was distracted stomping the unfortunate lad to mush, the other hunters ran in and finished it off. It was just another typical, successful hunt. Or so I thought.

As the survivors extracted the mangled mess that was once their friend from the mammoth's toes, I reminded them yet again that everyone dies sooner or later. But this time something new happened. Ordinarily the other hunters would have left the dead body to the hyenas, so I was taken by surprise when they didn't.

I was inside the mind of the particular hunter who made the radical decision to carry his dead comrade home, instead of carrying of an equally weighty chunk of mammoth brisket. I tried my best to tell him it was a bad decision given the meat shortage back at camp, but he was so convinced that he was right he was in sheer ecstasy. As far as he was concerned Sharmah was going to send his dead friend to this new afterlife place that everybody had been talking about the night before. That way his friend would come back to life, just like Sharmah had.

Back at camp, when this revolutionary proposal was put to Sharmah, I expected it to present the slacker with an impossible challenge, certain to bring about his undoing. But amazingly the smelly fellow rose to it for a change.

He knew from observing other people's reactions to rotting carcasses that a dead body apparently smelled worse than he did, and tended to bring wolves and bears sniffing around; so he imagined the body being far away from the tribe, deep inside an unused cave where smell wouldn't be an issue. The trouble was he didn't know of any unused caves since shelter from the elements was even harder to find than food was. All the caves in the area were occupied. Then he had the brainwave of his political life. Unselfish statesman that he was, he yielded his own dwelling to the corpse, thereby establishing the world's first burial tomb.

Acts of genuine altruism were still centuries away but on the face of it this surely looked like one. However, once I poked around in his scheme box I realised it was a lot less generous than it looked. The great man now had the keys to the kingdom (and the afterlife too apparently) so he reckoned he could live anywhere he damn well wanted – namely the main cave where all the women were. The decision didn't harm his self-esteem one bit.

The dead hunter was fifteen years old and by an amazing stroke of luck his father was still alive. The father, an elder about the same age as the chief still felt an emotional connection to his boy, and decided to fit him out appropriately for humanity's inaugural journey to the afterlife.

He put a spear in his son's right hand to hunt afterlife mammoths, and a flint knife in his left hand to cut afterlife meat. Everyone thought this was a great idea and stored it away for future use. Then they all looked to Sharmah for the next step.

Caught in the headlights Sharmah had to think fast. The pleasure of keeping his audience bumfuzzled by *spiritual* was still fresh in his mind from the night before, so he repeated the act to keep them further mystified. He closed his eyes and spoke to the spirits that lived in his newly invented afterlife, with all the seriousness he could muster. I'll say this for the young layabout: he knew how to play to his audience.

The crowd was utterly mesmerized by Sharmah's rambling since he had a nice voice and was saying new and interesting things. Just as interesting to the chief, and a lot more worrying, was the threat Sharmah now posed. Although he couldn't articulate it, the chief sensed an alarming need for something that a hundred thousand years later would be called separation of powers. Using nothing but words Sharmah had undermined the chief's absolute authority over the tribe that was now as likely to follow Sharmah as himself. A second focus of power had suddenly arisen. It was a worrying development, and the chief sensed it, but he also knew that he only ruled at the pleasure of his tribe, which a spear in the back could interrupt at anytime, so he was loath to make an issue of it. Had he done so, I think humanity would have looked quite differently today. Meantime I pricked up my imaginary ears.

I was on the inside and I suddenly understood why the crowd loved Sharmah's waffle so much. For you to understand it too, you have to remember that these guys were dead tired. That morning they'd chased and butchered half a ton of mammoth meat. That afternoon they'd carried it almost ten miles back to the cave, taking forty man-trips to complete the task. Meanwhile the women had been filling and hauling dozens of bear bladders full of water up from the river – an equally tough job given the slippery slopes they had to negotiate. Then, after burning some of the meat and eating it, they'd carried their dead comrade for a mile from the main cave across muddy patches and loose rock to Sharmah's recently surrendered cave. There they'd lain the corpse in the deepest part of the cave, and collected enough big rocks to block the cave's entrance.

These folks weren't just tired they were utterly exhausted – so exhausted that by the time Sharmah took centre stage they were quite happy to let him do all their thinking for them. If Sharmah said their dead tribesman was going to a better place; he was going to a better place. It was all just fine by them. Sharmah said so; it had to be true. As for the folks at the back who weren't listening or had fallen asleep, or didn't like the dead guy anyway, they simply didn't care if it was true or not. It was easier to go with the flow. After all, what harm could it do to play along? He-he, what indeed?

I witnessed this world-changing event from the inside and, well, *carpe diem* I say. When the Great Random drops gold into your lap, you grab it with both... well, I don't have hands but you get my drift. It was the opportunity I'd been waiting for to steal the limelight away from my rivals.

Here at last was something I could use; something I hadn't noticed before. People were always happy with the answer that suited them at the time, and would invariably declare it to be the correct one irrespective of veracity. Tired, worn out, bullied, or just mentally lazy, people simply decided the right answer was the one that caused them the least hassles. Truth had nothing to do with it.

This opened up endless possibilities for me. While the tribe's guard was down, and its many torpid minds were basking in the pleasure of charismatic gobbledygook, I quietly eased myself into the chemical mix and reinvented myself.

I had done this only once before with the pleasure of being right, but this time I came out not as the pleasure of being right *about dying*, I came out as the pleasure of being right *about passing over to the afterlife when you actually died*. In short I had become *spiritual*. I still didn't know what it meant, but neither did anyone else. They just loved the feeling that came with it.

Back at the burial the effect was staggering; I became a thought-sensation overnight. Everyone wanted to run me through their minds over and over just to get a hit. The entire tribe was suddenly high on the idea that the afterlife was available to everyone. Moreover it didn't have to be understood to be enjoyed. All that mattered was that they would feel good when they thought about it. Sharmah understood the afterlife. He'd been there. He knew it inside and out. It was good enough for them. Everyone else just had to pretend they understood and they got the same hit. They didn't need details. That was Sharmah's territory. And if anyone really wanted more details they could simply download them straight from the man himself. Sharmah had become the Google of 100,000 BC.

I found this total acceptance by the crowd utterly mesmerizing because something really interesting was going on. They were bonding more closely than ever, as if they'd become members of an exclusive club. The tribe itself was already a kind of club and you'd think that would have been good enough. But this was different. This was a club within a club, like a sub-society whose members had a secret handshake or who all knew where the body was buried – which in this case happened to be true.

I'd seen this joy of membership happen only once before, when a lost family from across the river had been allowed to join the tribe. Their feeling of acceptance had been wonderful to observe, but I never expected to see it again because most strays were usually sent packing for lack of resources to support them. But now the entire tribe was sharing the same kind of joy of acceptance. Being part of a unified group was apparently important to these people regardless of what united them. Unity seemed to reduce their anxiety. I could use that. So would others down the ages, incidentally, but none as effectively as I.

Back in the main cave, Sharmah's word was now second only to the chief's, and for some folks it was first. One fellow by the name of Horan believed so completely in Sharmah's infallibility that he felt more elated than at any time during his entire short life, including the time he'd been buggered by his best friend's father in the tall grass when they were supposed to be stalking game.

Believing in Sharmah made Horan feel so good, and his belief seemed to be so risk-free (it certainly didn't involve gravel knee or ants in his hair) that he decided to bind himself to Sharmah forever by devoting his life to the great man. He offered himself to Sharmah as a willing apprentice in the sure and certain knowledge he would learn great secrets from his mentor. Sharmah accepted of course, since it meant even less work and more prestige.

And so it came to pass that the first disciple in history was born. After that, Sharmah and Horan became inseparable; sometimes literally.

This is when I realised that pleasure was a great motivator of self-esteem. But I was also keenly aware that for pleasure to remain... well... pleasurable, it would need frequent refreshing, otherwise whatever had stimulated the pleasure would eventually get boring.

I'd seen this phenomenon in many aspects of human life already – most notably in sex, food, and chosen partners. What starts out as a seemingly inexhaustible source of delight eventually becomes anticipated, expected and just plain ho-hum. Even the best things in life, it seems, stop being the best after awhile. You probably already know what I mean, but I'll give you an example just in case. To avoid an X-rating, I'll use food.

I can still remember how good these folks thought a boiled potato was when they discovered how to boil water (not an easy thing to do without a metal pot, by the way). But when someone worked out that hot rocks thrown into bear-hide buckets full of water would make the water boil, it wasn't long before all sorts of foods got thrown in with them. The utterly inedible and sometimes toxic potato suddenly became a delicacy reserved only for special occasions. Then, a few years later, it became a bit of an indulgence for days when game was sparse. A few years after that, it became a staple food because it kept well in cold caves and could be boiled at will. Eventually the spud became so common no one would touch one unless a barbecued mammoth steak was wrapped around it. Then, as now, novelties didn't last long.

The same can be said for sexual positions, spouses' quirky noses, and friends' clever jokes, to name just a few, and rather than offend sensitive readers by touching raw nerves unnecessarily, I'll simply say that all decadent things move across the same spectrum from ecstasy at one end to mediocrity at the other once the initial excitement wears off.

So, back to the pleasure of having an afterlife to which everyone was invited, courtesy of Sharmah-the-charlatan, I needed it to flourish, so I started associating every pleasurable idea I could think of in the hope of keeping it new and interesting.

Here are just three of the many ideas I accreted to the afterlife, which worked then and still work today:

1. The afterlife is mysterious. The night sky is mysterious. Obviously the afterlife is in the sky. Mm, that felt good.

2. Arick the hunter (for example) who just died, was a good guy. He gets an ornamental spear and a flint knife for the afterlife; maybe a fox fur too if it's winter. Hardik on the other hand was screwing my wife. He gets a blunt stick and no coat. Ha! That'll teach him. Double mm.

3. Food is scarce in winter; the afterlife spirits must be angry. Let's do a trade – a young girl's virginity for a herd of mammoths. Me first! Mm, really liked that! Might make it an annual.

Let me say in my defence that not all the pleasurable ideas I accreted were violent, vindictive or sleazy. Some were quite quaint and nice: like leaving colourful flowers in the tombs, or leaving perfectly good food when it was plentiful, and so on. And I even helped people think up nice stories about what to expect in the afterlife, such as easy women and slow-moving game for men; and clean warm caves free of children and men, for women. Kids didn't need me at all. They simply imagined no grownups to boss them around, all by themselves. Kids have simple minds; they know exactly what they want. I would use this later.

But by and large, I have to say that most of the pleasurable ideas popping up in people's heads linking the afterlife to worldly behaviours had a slightly nasty tinge about them. I don't think it was because people were inherently nasty or vengeful. They could have been if they wanted to, and some were of course. But I think the reason was that being nasty 24/7 is hard work and most people really aren't that committed. No, I think the reason people then and now were quick to imagine bad things for their fellow man was because fear played a bigger role in human lives than they cared to admit.

From the privileged inside perspective that I have, I can see that everyone is frightened to some degree about this, that or the other – be it where the next meal might be coming from; or whether there's a snake in the grass; or will the tribe from the next valley attack while we're out hunting; or is the wife flirting with the gardener, and so forth.

Fear is nature's constant reminder that something or someone is surely waiting in the shadows to take advantage of your weaknesses. Such thoughts can wreak havoc on self-esteem, so a counter measure is essential to stay a step ahead. One counter measure is to fight fear with fear. Give people something more terrifying to fear than the horror movies playing out in your own head. Make up stories about ghastly things that will happen to them if they don't behave. And to reinforce it all, tell them how much worse it might get when they're dead. That'll get keep them distracted and worried.

Fear features heavily in my story later, because I couldn't have gotten to where I am today without it, but for the moment let me say that the importance of fear is very much downplayed by the human mind.

To protect their self-esteem, people like to pretend that fear is just one emotion in a smorgasbord of emotions from which they can pick and choose when it suits them. Many even believe that it's a primitive throwback of evolution to a time when the world really was a jungle, and will eventually be cast onto the scrap heap of superfluous evolutionary stepping-stones; like gills and tails.

Love, some say, is the real driving force in life. Without love there can be no tribe; no community; no civilization. Others claim love conquers all, including fear. Indeed I've heard it said that everything humans do can be traced back to one of these two emotions; fear or love. It's a nice idea, and it comforts many people to believe that, but having observed humans from the inside I have to say that from where I sit there is only one emotion: fear. Everything people do is rooted in fear, whether they know it or not.

Yes everything. Even love.

What! I hear you say. How can love, that most noble of emotions that brings out everything good and decent in humanity be rooted in fear? Well, quite easily actually if you view it off its pedestal. Love is really just a clever survival response to fear – specifically, the fear of being alone; the fear of not being able to go through life without someone else's help.

By the way, I'm not trying to belittle love, just explain it. Love is actually very important to me since it helps propagate my hosts, and long may it continue. I have marvelled at the pleasure it brings to its practitioners – albeit often at the expense of good sense – but everything in life is a trade off. A mum-to-be who fears having to raise a helpless child all by herself; or a dad who fears some punk might steal his wife and kill his child will both experience those fears as love for each other, united in the cause of making sure none of those awful things happen. In doing so they get one of the best pleasure hits that life has to offer. And jolly good luck to them, I say. It's usually rewarded with regular sex anyway, so no wonder people like it.

Indeed love is apparently so nice it has become habitual in many people just so they can continuously experience the joy it brings, and they'll practise it their entire lives – love junkies you might say. For others love is just a way of getting what they want, by snuggling up to a generous provider for a larger piece of the pie. It's a good way of cooperating with a potential rival in a kind of win-win arrangement. Fair enough too. Mutual cooperation beats selfish competition any day, and two heads are usually better one; except under a guillotine of course.

So love, I agree, conquers a lot of things. But not all things. When the chips are down; with death knocking on the door, and comfy space in the afterlife scarce, it's every man and women for themselves. This is when gaining access to the afterlife demands some serious refocusing on whom you say you love. In this situation the smart ones always include the priest holding the keys to the afterlife.

Speaking of mums-to-be (which I was a while back) it was a mum from this very tribe who struck on another idea that fitted nicely into my portfolio.

Her snotty nosed six-year-old called Orlap was up to his usual skylarking, giving his sister Larna a hard time.

'Orlap!' shouted mum, 'if you push your sister onto the fire once more Sharmah won't let you into the afterlife.'

But Orlap just pushed Larna anyway and shouted at the top of his voice, 'THERE'S NO SUCH PLACE AS THE AFTERLIFE! IT'S ALL MAMMOTH POO!'

A couple of mothers within earshot raised their ample eyebrows and tut-tutted under their fetid breaths, while mum herself was mortified at her son's blatant blasphemy. If word got out that her son was a non believer, well... it didn't bear thinking about. She grabbed Orlap by the hair, pulled down his elk-hide shorts and gave him a well deserved hiding.

I was inside mum's head when she justified the walloping, and here is what she was thinking: *It's for your own good you little stinker! Don't you dare say you don't believe in the great Sharmah or his afterlife! If he knew, he might never allow us in!*

Orlap was as thick as mammoth hair, and missed the point of the spanking completely, but the upside was he never pushed his sister into the fire again. He would of course get his mum's point eventually after more beatings specifically consequential to his outspoken blasphemy, but I twigged on straight away and loved it. I immediately attached mum's message as a corollary for believing in the afterlife.

The way that worked was this: if you said you didn't believe in the afterlife, you wouldn't be allowed in, even if you arrived at the mouth of the great celestial cave feeling rather foolish and contrite. Too bad. You said you didn't believe when you had the chance, now you have to stay behind for the hyenas to munch on. No cushy afterlife; just hyena chow.

Word soon got around and suddenly I was attracting recruits like flies to wolf scat. Everyone was talking – not just about how important it was to believe, but how important is was to *say* you believed. It followed then, that if you wanted a place in the afterlife, people likely to be at your burial had to know that's want you wanted. And the way they got to know was by you crowing loudly about how much you believed, while you were still alive. Only true believers got in, so obviously everyone had to know you were a true believer.

Then the competitive side of human nature kicked in. People decided that the more they believed in the afterlife, the better the perks they would get when they arrived. Everything they said and did while they were alive to demonstrate their unquestioning faith raised them up one rung in the great celestial hierarchy.

With an incentive like this, I spread more widely that Herpes, not just throughout this tribe but throughout all other tribes we met from time to time. The best part of the arrangement was that I got paid both coming and going. Not only did I spread through the ranks of true believers who were competing to prove who was more worthy, but anyone who dared question me got very short shrift. And anyone foolish enough to suggest that the pleasures of the afterlife didn't actually exist got shunned by the tribe (at best) until they changed their mind, or at worst got tied to a tree as bear bait if they didn't.

Here was something new that in hindsight I should have been able to predict. People were prepared to defend any feel-good belief – to the death if necessary – rather than give up that belief for the sake of the boring truth.

They led pretty shitty lives most of the time anyway, given they were weak, vulnerable and tasty in a world apparently designed to eat them, so they didn't really have much to look forward to while they were alive. Then suddenly Sharmah comes along and gives them something wonderful to look forward to when they're dead. They certainly weren't going to let that go without a fight.

And even if the occasional someone had an epiphany and realised it was all bollocks, they quickly suppressed such thoughts since there was nothing better on the horizon to replace it. An afterlife was the nicest thing that was ever going to happen to them. It was easy to see why they got angry with anyone who threatened the illusion. That hasn't changed.

Converts skyrocketed while disbelievers plummeted. I was on a roll. By simply teaming up with the pleasure of believing you're right, and by inference, reinforcing the anger of being doubted, I suddenly found myself close to the top of the heap. I now virtually ruled human brains in almost everything they did. They were so addicted to the joy of being spiritual, that I had no trouble permeating every thought and deed they could execute. Moreover, with a bit of tweaking, anything they could poke a stick at could be considered spiritual – a concept I've brought all the way into the present day.

If you don't believe me, take a look at a beautiful maple tree in autumn, or a sunset in full blaze, or a rainbow in all its glory. Don't they make you feel good? Don't you feel spiritual? That's me doing that. Or gaze up at the stars next time you're out at night. Stars are just about the most hostile gobs of burning hell that nature has ever concocted, but I've got you staring at them all gaga in spiritual wonderment. No need to thank me; all part of the service.

Life had become pretty good for me and I probably should have left it there. I'd done all right. I'd gone from a simple bad-news thought about inevitable death, to a controlling influence in everything people did. It was a magnificent achievement in anyone's books and in hindsight I should have left it there. The trouble was I'd been bouncing around inside human brains for so long that I'd taken on one of its curses: I was never satisfied. Sure I was now boss cocky of the folding brain, but your skull contains more than just grey matter. Indeed grey matter is just the icing. I wanted the white matter underneath – the whole cake as it were. But to get at it I had to make a deal with Primeval Fear.

Primal Fear – lucky bastard, at least he had a name – was still the head of your head. His power was, and is, the holy grail of mind manipulation. When I first became aware of Primal Fear he'd already been around forever living deep below my part of the brain, in a little cave called the amygdala, to which I as a resident of the lofty neocortex had no direct access. You see, when Primal Fear bursts out of its cave, e.g. when a spider lands on your arm, or a snarling wolf jumps out at you with lips peeled back ready for dinner, I get completely bypassed.

The whole neocortex including yours truly gets locked into a holding pattern so Primal Fear can get you running as fast as you can, hopefully to survive another day. I'm not complaining, mind. That's the way it's supposed to work. On my own I'm far too intellectual to be a survival instinct. If I'd been put in charge when Mrs Wolf sized you up, I'd have had you trying to negotiate a deal with her; to have a chat about alternative diets; to suggest there were other tastier animals in the forest to eat.

But Primal Fear was more experienced. He (if you'll permit the barefaced anthropomorphism) had honed his skills over eons and eons down to two simple alternatives: stick around to fight it out, or run as fast as you can, or at least a bit faster than your companions.

Most of the time it was run as fast as you can, and even then most of the time you got eaten; but not always. Obviously enough of you must have survived to pass Primal Fear on to your offspring as a useful survival tactic. The people who paid most attention to Primal Fear thus went on to make other kids who did the same; and by inference: those that didn't, didn't.

Primal Fear was therefore a better survivor-maker than I could ever be. Consequently I wanted to find out more about him; to see if I could strike a deal and join forces. Trouble was he would slip back into his cave so quickly after he'd finished his work that I never got a chance to have a decent conversation.

But all that was about to change.

6

POOR QUALITY CONTROL

Let's now jump forward seventy thousand years to 30,000 BC. Of course nobody calls it that because C still hasn't happened, but you know when I mean. By now everyone over the age of five knows they are going to die sooner or later, and no matter what misery life throws at them on this mortal coil, they'll be warm and snug in Sharmah's afterlife. Apart from the secret of making fire, there wasn't one other piece of information that had travelled down through the ages as robustly as the myth of the afterlife – thanks to me.

Since the days when Sharmah grabbed his audience and got the ball rolling, a whole industry had grown up around the idea that priestly types like Sharmah were the chosen gatekeepers to the afterlife, who knew the secret of getting in. What had started as a gig for keeping Sharmah-the-lazy fat, happy and sexually satisfied had become a worldwide business for thousands of likewise ambitious priests. Its phenomenal success through the ages lay in the serendipitous happenstance (serendipitous for the priests that is) that the only way to reach the afterlife was to give the priest exactly what he wanted, even if that included food, warm pelts or your youngest daughter.

As a consequence, the status game had hotted up, which is to say the better you treated the priest, the more he might like you, and the better the deckchair you could expect on the Good Ship Afterlife. Similarly, the more lavish the offerings people left in your burial cave, the more comfortable you would be when you arrived.

The blindingly obvious corollary to all this was that the more stuff you owned in this world, the better the deal you got in the next. In other words, the afterlife had somehow developed a class system.

As far as I'm aware, I had nothing to do with this arrangement. If I had thought of it I'd have been into it like sand at a beach orgy; but in all honesty I can't claim credit. The human mind, I was learning, had an insatiable propensity for feathering its own nest, and was quite happy saying or doing whatever it felt like to get whatever it wanted. With a greed-based process like that on my side, rapid evolution was inevitable. I spread virtually everywhere.

The only downside (if I should describe it so) was that language was evolving even more rapidly than I was, so I was being spread around with virtually no quality control whatsoever.

Different forms of me were popping up all over the place with increasingly outrageous promises attached. For example if you lived in a desert, the afterlife was a cool, lush, green garden brimming with ripe fruit and roast lamb. But you could only get there if you gave nice things like ripe fruit and roast lamb to the priest and his apprentices to eat while you were still alive.

If you lived in the Arctic Circle, the afterlife was a warm moist place with salmon steaks and whale blubber aplenty, but entry was limited to people who donated warm clothes and firewood to the Medicine Man.

There were plenty of other examples, but my personal favourite was dreamed up by a nation of huge redheaded brutes living in Scandinavia, who called their particular afterlife Valhalla. These chaps had serious imagination.

Valhalla was apparently a continent-sized hall with a roof made of spear shafts and fighting- shields, both of which dripped gold and diamonds. In this wonderful place, your recently dead worldly enemies would attend to your every need, from washing your feet to cooking your pheasants to pickling your herring to crushing your grapes, all the while keeping the fire well stoked.

Of course when the priest told this story to his worshipers, he sidestepped the glaringly obvious contradiction that enmity is a two-way street, so *your* enemy would surely regard you as *their* enemy, and thus expect identical treatment. But ever-prepared, if anyone dared to mention it, the priest could weasel his way around that little conundrum by saying that in a battle with your enemies, whoever died last got the best deal. As a sweetener he would add that dying with a sword in your hand meant that you were the obvious victor, which was pretty patriotic stuff given their national pastime was hacking people to pieces anyway.

But as usual, humans are never satisfied with just one version of any story. Eventually debate raged about what Valhalla really looked like; and some seriously violent spats occurred between rival tribes over what I considered to be quite trivial matters; but they saw otherwise. For example relatively close tribes – both culturally and geographically – would happily go to war against each other over whether the gold and diamonds dripping from Valhalla ceiling dripped from the spear shafts or from the shields. Weighty matters indeed.

Since human dissatisfaction knows no bounds, eventually people began demanding more from their priests than the standard mumbo jumbo mixed with chicken entrails that they'd been getting for millennia. The whole act needed a makeover, and just like in Sharmah's day, the priests delivered.

Since everyone had a different view of me by now anyway, the priests played on this theme. They made up stories about rain spirits and lightning spirits and season spirits and drought spirits and river spirits and you-name-it spirits, to accentuate their exclusive understanding of the forces at work, which required deep insight beyond the intellectual grasp of the average person.

If you expected clear proof of the forces surrounding the afterlife you were out of luck. Such forces were no longer considered natural, they were supernatural. Real proof was impossible for mere mortals to understand. But if you needed some basic evidence (an expectation I actively discouraged since it was impossible to deliver on) then you needed look no further than the life-force inside the snake or the ox or the bison, or whatever beast was handy.

Life-force, priests now said, was inexplicable and unknowable by non-priests. It was drawn from the afterlife when you were born and sent back to the afterlife when you died – so don't get too bloody nosey or you'll experience it well before you might want to!

To prove that life-force was now in the custody of priests, one talented fellow I'd been watching for some time drew a pretty good likeness of a bison on a cave wall in France. The drawing was so realistic that when light from the torch flickered on it, everyone expected the bison to run right off the wall and out of the cave. When it didn't, everyone asked why.

The priest proclaimed the bison couldn't run away because he had taken the beast's life spirit and was holding it inside his own body giving him great power. The force of life was a spirit, so obviously all living things contained spirits until they died whereupon the spirit returned to – yep, you guessed it – the afterlife, or if you were really hip in 30,000 BC, to the *spirit world*. This proof was a nice sounding but circular argument that simply occupied time and explained nothing; but when delivered skilfully, the audience soaked it up. You're welcome.

Such snazzy doubletalk still runs riot today whenever something can't be explained. Instead of saying *I don't know, let's think about it, form a hypothesis, test it with observations and then validate it as a theory; or start again if we're wrong,* most people prefer to jabber on as if they are experts until they've proved one equals one and everyone's forgotten what the original question was. The really clever ones just make up a new name for an old problem so they can bamboozle their pesky questioners with jargon. As in:

'Why do some people sneeze when they step out into bright sunlight?'

'It's because they've got photosensitivity.'

'What's photosensitivity?'

'It's something that some people have. It makes them sneeze when they go into bright sunlight.'

'Ah! It's caused by photosensitivity. Yes I see that now.'

No new knowledge is added; just a new word giving the illusion of knowledge to another satisfied customer.

Of course, I'm right in there encouraging such circular arguments. The last thing I want is for some smart-ass to figure out that the only honest line on my resume is that they're going to die one day. That would be no fun at all.

If you've been paying attention you'll have noticed that I haven't yet answered the original question: How did I get an audience with Primal Fear? I'm coming to that (you'd hope so) and it has to do with logic.

Logic was another idea that had popped up recently and was growing legs. It was still a baby and hadn't made any real inroads as a puppeteer, but it was useful from time to time. The logic of the day went like this:

Bison alive. Bison got spirit inside. Me alive. Therefore me got spirit inside.

The logic was impeccable, but as someone would say thirty thousand years later, logic is a measure of consistency, not of validity. Guided by this newfound logic, it followed (logically) that good people had good spirits in them and bad people had bad spirits in them.

Back then, good and bad meant pretty much the same things that they mean today, namely, good means *agrees with you*, bad means *disagrees with you*.

Different versions of language found it useful to describe this concept more succinctly, namely as *right* and *wrong* respectively. Thus, when a mob of good people came across a bad person, it was the duty of the former to change the latter's bad spirit into a good one. To do that, good spirit had to have a chat with bad spirit, and to do that, good spirit had to get bad spirit's attention. It was the right thing to do.

An effective way of getting a bad person's attention was to hit them with materials denser than their flesh, such as sticks, stones, and animal bones. If that didn't work, testing their ability to breathe underwater was another favourite; and if that didn't work, setting them on fire always got their undivided attention. Gruesome? Yes. But the right thing to do.

It was during one of those times – when one unfortunate wretch was screaming her smoke-filled lungs out while trying to flee the burning stake she was tied to – that I was able to observe Primal Fear over a long period.

It takes anything from three minutes to two hours (amazingly) for a human to burn to death, depending on the ambient temperature, the bloodlust driving the crowd, and not surprisingly whether its raining or not. But on average, five minutes will do it. This was heaps of time for me to mingle with Primal Fear.

I first tried attracting his attention inside the victim's mind, strongly advising the poor darling that she'd feel so much better if she changed from being bad to being good. But she was screaming so loudly she wouldn't pay attention; so I left her to it. As luck would have it, Primal Fear was flooding through her spectators' minds too.

These folks had a lot more time to revise their opinions of right and wrong, and many had already come around to the priest's opinion, especially those next in line for the bonfire. All were eager to avoid refuelling the gruesome entertainment.

While Primal Fear was pumping terror through their minds and bodies, I was in there too reinforcing the notion that right and wrong was really just a question of who owned the matches. If torch-bearing thugs with more firewood than brains expected some kiss-ass, I strongly recommended puckering-up. Martyrs were no use to me; I needed walking talking survivors to spread me about, otherwise how could I possibly make use of Primal Fear's awesome power?

To my surprise and delight, Primal Fear didn't seem to mind what I did while he was working. It turned out that he was a pretty simple soul with the ambition of a roof tile. Despite his awesome power of total command and control over everything that people did in a crisis, he only ever exercised it when he absolutely had to: during real honest-to-god life and death situations. Otherwise he didn't care what was going on.

Primal Fear had the power to frighten the bejesus out of the most fearless hunters on Earth; he could get the most clay-footed oaf carrying a stolen bear cub to break the record for the hundred yard dash; and he could even bleach a healthy man's hair white overnight if the fright was large enough. Yet he never bothered to capitalize on it. As soon as the danger had gone, so was he. He hadn't changed in the slightest way in over a million years; what a tragic waste of evolution.

After watching Primal Fear in action, I realized I could never strike a deal with him nor mimic his awesome power, so there was no point trying. But I did figure out what could bring him out of his cave – me! I could draw him out; I just had to frame myself properly. Since people already knew they were going to die one day, all I had to do was convince them they were going to die there and then, and out would pop Primal Fear ready to do what he does best.

For example if Zoran-the-disembowler (not his real name) pointed a dagger at you and demanded four goats per year in tax, I would then play a colour movie in your head showing your grey intestines sliding out of your white belly through a scarlet gash he'd recently put there. If the movie was realistic enough, Primal Fear would leap up and scare the daylights out of you to get you ready to run away.

But before you started running, I would burst in like Superman and propose an alternative solution: just agree with Zoran-t-d; suck it up, and your spleen would stay where it belonged. My new golden rule was: whoever holds the knife makes the rules.

The more I encouraged people to think that way, the more survivors survived to host me. And it worked. It worked back then and it still works today. This is how it goes: when a simple change of mind means staying alive – change your mind. See? You're already thinking about it aren't you? Next time it comes up for real, I'll remind you.

Using this technique of manipulating Primal Fear, I found that I could change minds much faster than my original non-specific reminder about death being inevitable. I would tell them death was immediate. And the better I got at it, the more I spread around.

So, at last, after a million years of patient, plodding practice I was almost ready to rule the world. Almost.

All I needed was a name.

7

JARGON WITH A CAPITAL G

It is now about 2,000 BC, or roughly four thousand years before I would force this unfortunate typist to tap out my story on his keyboard; and a lot has happened since we last spoke. As I recall, I had just started helping people decide between right and wrong based on what was going to keep them alive versus what was going to kill them. I played with this theme a lot during the intervening twenty-seven thousand years, and learned two valuable lessons: evolution works but it's unpredictable; and children mostly believe what adults tell them. I'll try to explain.

The more I got into manipulating minds, the more I realized that people weren't as gullible as I'd first thought, with some people being surprisingly resistant and hostile to new ideas, even ideas that could save their lives. As far as I could tell there was nothing wrong with telling them they were going to die one day – it made perfectly good sense – but not everyone coped the same way.

Take the time when I reminded King Sargon of Akkad that he was going to die one day, and if he wanted to know how much his subjects really loved (i.e. feared) him before the big day arrived then he would have to make them show it. His reaction was to insist each father in the kingdom must sacrifice his firstborn son in the king's regal honour. It was a pretty radical reaction and it had some pretty surprising consequences.

King Sargon was a nasty piece of work at the best of times – the best of times being when he was taxing only half of what everyone produced. The worst of times were when they wouldn't pay.

Sargon was already an interesting character for several reasons by the time I started to take notice of him. To begin with, he was the illegitimate son of a priestess. Yes, I said priestess – female. Even women were in on the afterlife gate keeping act by now, although still subject to male dominance of course (more on this later).

Secondly, Sargon was the first wannabe world conqueror that humankind can claim to have produced. Of course world domination was far too grand an ambition given he had no idea how big the world was, but you have to give him points for trying. He never succeeded in that goal of course, but in pitching his ambition so high he started a tedious fad that still continues. Indeed Sargon should really be as famous as Constantine or Napoleon or Hitler or Bush-the-Dopier, but in reality hardly anyone's ever heard of him, much less cares.

In his heyday Sargon of Akkad was more feared than leprosy, yet he is a virtual unknown today. I didn't know it at the time but I've since discovered that given enough time, all wannabe world dominators eventually get cast onto the scrap heap of *never-heard-of-them* along with almost everyone else. Almost. A select few special people's names make it into the vernacular despite the odds, and you'll probably know most of them when I mention them later. Why? Because they were memorable. Special. They were all virulent carriers and disseminators of me. They feature later in my story so I won't spoil the surprise, but suffice to say a select few including the forgotten Sargon have had a bigger impact on you than you might care to admit. They made you what you are, i.e. a potent carrier of me.

But back to Sargon himself – he was also interesting to me for another reason. When his high-priestess mother realised she was up the duff with him courtesy of her randy palace gardener who liked to plant more than just olive trees, she hid herself away from all but a few of her trusted but ultimately doomed handmaidens until baby Sargon was born. But she couldn't stay hidden forever.

To preserve her self-esteem after the cord was cut, she put the little chap in a basket of reeds lined with bitumen to make the basket waterproof, in preparation for floating it away. Despite there being no tarmac roads back then, bitumen was surprisingly plentiful. On hot days there were naturally occurring puddles of the stuff all over Middle Eastern deserts, as indeed there still are today, which explains why oil companies would decide the Middle East was a great place to look for oil four thousand years later. But I digress.

Once the basket was waterproof, the high-priestess's penultimate act was to cast baby Sargon adrift down the Euphrates River.

Sound vaguely familiar?

Yes, I'm sure it does if you change the name of the river to the Nile and the country to Egypt. But remember this was two thousand years before the Moses you know and love supposedly got the same treatment, and should serve as a lesson to you all that history isn't always what your Sunday School teacher taught you.

A little further downstream Baby Sargon got miraculously discovered by a newly appointed handmaiden sent there to await his appearance. The wee and somewhat wet lad was then brought to the high priestess who feigned surprise at the discovery and declared publicly that the gods had miraculously sent her a child to raise. She would therefore care for the baby as if it were her own son, which of course he was. It wasn't quite the virgin birth story that would eventually float to the top of the list of improbable excuses for unwanted babies, but it was definitely a precursor.

Incidentally, if you're wondering what the high-priestess's final act was after casting little Sargon adrift in the basket, it was to have all her original handmaidens and midwives killed so the secret wouldn't get out, which is where you get the expression *keeping mum* (no not really – I just made that up to remind you to be sceptical about what you read).

So if everyone who knew about the secret was killed, how did the secret eventually get out? When Sargon grew up into the spoilt little brat he was always going to be, he got curious about his family tree, and pressed a rather sharp copper knife against his mommy's belly to find out who his real dad was. She quite sensibly took my advice (see earlier) and spilled the beans to avoid spilling her innards.

As for how Sargon became famous: a lucky break and a suspicious nature saw him survive an assassination attempt. The botched attempt was made in the Palace of Uruk by the king of that region while Sargon was visiting on what he believed to be a diplomatic mission on behalf of his own king back at Akkad. Feeling very annoyed by the attempt, Sargon slaughtered everyone in Uruk palace plus a few neighbours who'd run in to see what the ruckus was all about; but not before extracting the vital bit of information as to who had set him up.

It turned out the mastermind was his own king, the King of Akkad who was secretly envious of Sargon's youth and strength. Who'd have thought eh? Shakespeare couldn't have done better.

So, feeling quite a bit less loyal toward his own king now, he returned home to Akkad and despatched everyone living in that palace too. Two kings in one week – no wonder he got a swelled head. Being the last man standing in two palaces in two adjoining nations, Sargon glimpsed his destiny and declared himself king of everywhere, then systematically went about making it so. Within five years he'd conquered all of Asia Minor – which is when I decided to get involved.

As I mentioned, Sargon, like all despots since, began to wonder just how much his subjects really loved him. He was already feared more than snakebite, so to quantify things more precisely he (and I) demanded absolute obedience from everyone by insisting they dispatch their firstborns.

We both expected instant compliance from the lesser hordes, but oddly they didn't take to the notion of sacrificing their children a hundred percent. Sargon was livid so I suggested he order his henchmen to start beheading the recalcitrant parents too, my logic being that if evolution worked, dead disobedient parents weren't going to keep producing disobedient offspring, and therefore the general population of disobedient people should eventually go down while the population of obedient ones should go up.

My thinking was right of course, but life being the great waterbed that it is, nothing happens in isolation. My idea just left a lot of obedient but unsupported orphans begging in the streets. So what, you ask? Well so did I. But it turns out that the downside of increasing the beggar population is that beggars don't pay tax; and tax was the whole purpose of the exercise in the first place. Ironic, wouldn't you say? As I said, evolution works, but you can't always predict the outcome.

King Sargon himself came up with a better solution than mine. He simply reframed the instruction, using the *threat* of something horrible happening whenever you were least expecting it. Instead of *kill your firstborn to show you love me*, he said *kill your firstborn or else henchmen will come knocking in the dead of night and do it for you plus any siblings they might encounter in the process; and if you're not home the gods that I control will shower plague and pestilence upon your whole family wherever they are. Either way the afterlife will be denied you for all eternity.*

I mean really! I should have thought of that myself. It was more or less what I'd been saying for thousands of years anyway, and it shows how much I'd taken my eye off the ball. That's what absolute power does to you.

Speaking of gods, which Sargon did a lot once he decided he was one, god was a word I didn't take to at first. It's a lazy word that doesn't really convey the true mystery of what the human imagination can dream up.

But, sadly, the word had been catching on, and there wasn't much I could do about it.

In my defence let me say that I couldn't keep my eye on everyone and everything all the time. I was inside about twenty million heads by now, which took quite a bit of coordination, and some things were bound to slip through the cracks. Unfortunately language was one of them.

Language really got away from me because people were such insatiable blabbermouths. Honestly, they never shut up – some not even when they were asleep – and they were making up new jargon on a daily basis. I wasn't really in charge of language anyway, the Great Random was, which is to say, no one was, so language took on a life of its own. If I'd had a name, maybe I could have taken charge, but I didn't, so I didn't.

Jargon itself wasn't a new thing of course. Sensible jargon had been around for eons, even in Muktuk's day, but it was supposed to be used purely for survival reasons. Obviously, yelling out: *Raak, move your legs rapidly in the direction opposite to the large spotted cat that is moving its legs rapidly towards you with its tooth-lined digestive tract agape* took far too long to say. Surely *Run! Leopard!* was much more economical to say and much more likely to be passed down from survivor to survivor. Jargon used that way was a good thing.

But as tribes went their different ways up hill and down dale looking for greener pastures, jargon got completely out of hand – so much so that when tribes met up again after a few hundred years of separation, all dressed differently and whining about how much better things were in the good old days, they couldn't understand each other anymore. Jargon had turned into a completely new language, and the ensuing misunderstandings got quite ugly. Let me tell you there were some rip-roaring blood baths over that little evolutionary fuck-up, which I'd love to go into in more detail, but they're not really central to my story and might frighten the children.

The reason I mention jargon at all is because it shows what lazy blighters people were becoming. They were starting to use jargon in non-survival situations, which was always going to be a recipe for disaster. For example what was wrong with saying *spirits that emanate from the afterlife, which you'd better believe in or I'll feed you to the crocodiles*? It's a perfectly good, well-structured, meaningful description containing absolutely no ambiguity.

But no, some of the Bronze Age folks living by the Euphrates River thought it was quicker to say *gods* instead. Well of course it was quicker! But what's the bloody rush? That's the trouble with humans – always rushing. There's never enough time to do something right, but there's always plenty of time to do it wrongly three or four times. Moreover, a short word like god was always going to be subject to wholesale misunderstandings that a more lengthy description could never be.

Anyway, I lost that battle and pretty soon there were gods coming out of the woodwork: god of the sun, god of the moon, god of the planets (only the visible ones of course), god of love, god of war, god of this, god of that. And if that wasn't confusing enough, there could be demi-gods too: the offspring of gods and humans who'd been up to no good behind the bike shed. It all got out of control very quickly.

To illustrate one extreme of the god-saturation problem, one bunch of priests living east of Sumer had their peons enthralled with the notion that there were exactly nine million different gods, and if one person could name them all, the world would end and everyone would go to a better place. Why nine million? Why not ten million, or eight point six million? I don't really know. I have noticed that humans like round numbers, so that could explain part of it, but nine is only round at the top, so it isn't a completely satisfying explanation.

Anyway, it was nine million. Not that it could matter less what it was, because no one ever managed it. But I have to say it was one of the neater tricks I'd seen priests come up with, since their particular language had only about ten thousand words in it by this time, which meant naming the gods meant multiplying their vocabulary a thousandfold – a not insignificant achievement and surely the reason Sumerians went to all the trouble of inventing writing.

Writing was an essential component of this ludicrous exercise, otherwise by the time you got to god number two million, five hundred and twelve someone would come along and interrupt with, 'Hang on, I think you said that one already.' And definitively no one wanted to get to god eight million and four, have a memory lapse and have to start all over again. Writing was the only way it could work.

But nine million stone tablets came with their own logistical challenges that doomed the exercise from the start. Apart from taking something like twelve thousand years for one man (women weren't allowed) to make up the names and chisel them onto stone tablets, anyone who actually had a warehouse big enough to store all nine million was plagued by pilferers stealing the tablets for roof tiles.

Personally, I'm OK with this kind of mystical nonsense because it distracts people from thinking too much, but this particular concept was unhelpful to my cause. Nine million gods stretched my patience to breaking point, so I wound down my activity in their heads to an absolute minimum.

As it happened I had to abandon this lot on more fundamental grounds than bookkeeping practices. Their real crime in my eyes was that they kept denying that they were going to die one day. Despite what I kept telling them, they were utterly convinced that when someone looked like she was dead, she was merely passing over from her body into the body of something lower down the Natural Order to atone for bad behaviours committed in the current life. Personally I'd never seen such a passover happen, but I can't deny there were an awful lot of rats running around; so who knows?

The point is: my whole *raison d'etre* was founded on death being a one-way street with a tautological dead-end at the end of it, so this was a rebellion I couldn't win.

I left them to their strange delusions and concentrated elsewhere.

In hindsight it was a good decision because as things turned out, their descendants eventually got tired of god-naming and wrote down recipes for prawn vindaloo and naan bread instead; so it all balanced out nicely in the end.

By now you'll be thinking I've wandered off the track yet again, but I promise I will tell you how I got my name – eventually. But I have to give you a bit more background for it to make sense, and to do that we have to go back to Mesopotamia, to the bustling metropolis of Ur (once known as Uruk) in what you might now pronounce as Iraq, because that is where it happened.

Having invented the g-word, Mesopotamians were having a pretty good run at god-collecting. Before their civilization ran out of enthusiasm they had anything from seven hundred to two thousand gods on the books; and not just the celestial bodies I mentioned earlier. Every plant and animal was now a god. And not just the obvious ones like wheat and trees and cows and horses and tigers and snakes. Quite obtuse ones like yeast and mushrooms, beetles and baboons, and frogs and toads were also gods. And not just living things either. Inanimate objects were named as deities. And there were some real doozies that were just downright silly – an abuse of the word in my opinion – such as the god of flat beer, and the god of ceilings. I mean, come on – ceilings?

In fact they ended up with so many gods that I'm convinced that similar to what happened to the Sumerians, this over abundance of gods also had more to do with poor bookkeeping than high reverence. The same god whose image was copied over and over again could look quite different after a while depending on which side of the river you lived. For example the same god could easily end up with a slightly different face or symbol depending on how sharp or blunt the chisel was, how fine or coarse the sandstone block was, and of course how sober or drunk the mason was. Consequently, supposedly identical gods ended up with quite different faces and thus got different names. This turned out to be good old jargon at work again.

Keep two groups of Mesopotamians separated by the Euphrates River for a couple of decades and that's what happens: slightly different representations of what were supposed to be the same god would end up being called different gods.

To their credit, instead of killing each other over such disparities, as was the rest of the world's solution for similar disputes, these guys just decided the slightly different images were now different gods, and agreed to give them different names – proving yet again that the human brain's capacity for self-delusion may well be limitless (more about this later).

But such behaviour was really starting to annoy me; I was losing control. I'd been putting Primal Fear to good use all over Europe, in the Americas and throughout most of Greater Asia; but this little corner of Asia Minor was so bloated with gods that people no longer feared them. Instead they created them, owned them, controlled them. For example, if one particular rain god didn't come up to scratch by delivering drought instead of rain, the locals would just invent a new rain god and pray to it instead. Gods were a shekel a dozen, and had become all about the here and now, rather than their original purpose as the welcoming party of the afterlife.

Things were falling apart. Obviously I needed another Sharmah to get things back on track. But before I did, I would need a new angle. Then, tah-dah! I had the brainwave to end all brainwaves.

Despite the plethora of gods that the locals had dreamed up, it occurred to me they'd missed one – a god of gods. If people needed gods, surely gods also needed gods. But like the pyramid that can only have one apex, gods could only have one god. A god of gods was by definition the head honcho god – the *numero uno* of what must now be regarded as lesser deities. You can't have two gods of gods; they can't be gods of each other, *ergo* there can only be one god of gods. How clever was that?

But how to distinguish?

Ah-ha – a capital letter. The god of gods would be called God so there'd be no ambiguity. Brilliant. This was my way back in. It would work, I was sure of it. All I needed now was a Sharmah-like character to spread the word.

Initially I picked a guy who called himself Aaron, simply because I like to do things alphabetically; and since aardvarks didn't qualify, Aaron was first on the list. But it turned out Aaron had a stutter and his name was really just Aron, which put two strikes against him.

Abram was next on the list, and he turned out to be an excellent showman with ambition bigger than all outdoors. His arithmetic was pretty ordinary though, which didn't really matter that much but I mention it up front because you might have read somewhere that he used to tell everyone he was ninety-nine years old, which he clearly wasn't since he still had most of his teeth at a time when oral hygiene was about as fashionable as catching leprosy. Moreover, he believed he owned the land rights to the entire Middle East, and expected to populate it all by himself. You just don't see that kind of ambition in a ninety-nine year old.

For the record, his age miscalculation had arisen from the fact that the local people recognized only three seasons per year, namely summer, not-summer and inundation – the latter being when the Euphrates River flooded, drowning its valley and most of its slowest riverside dwellers. Usually this happened just once a year, but the melting snows of the Armenian Mountains were unpredictable phenomena at the best of times, and it wasn't unheard of to have two or three inundations during a single El Nino year.

Abram was already a good storyteller even before I picked him and he loved to interrupt conversations with, 'Ha! You think that's bad? Back in my day, twenty inundations ago...' Then he would hold his audience captive with stories of his exploits far and wide. Eventually someone with a head for numbers reckoned he had to be nearly a hundred to have done everything he claimed to have done.

Anyway, all age-references aside Abram was a truly masterful orator with a booming voice and good vocabulary. He smelled a lot better than Sharmah too, so his audience tended to gather closer, bolstering his self-esteem as a leader. Whilst I only put the idea into his head about there being a God of gods, Abram grabbed it and ran with it until all I could see were the soles of his sandals disappearing over the dunes. I'd have been perfectly happy if he'd just walked around chatting to people, spreading me one-on-one. But no, that wasn't Abe's style at all. Abe had plans. Abe was a man in a hurry – another characteristic atypical in a ninety-nine year old. To illustrate, here is the spiel he would tell people in town squares.

'When I was ninety years old and nine, the one true God, the God of gods, whose name cannot be spoken, appeared to me, and said unto me, I am the Almighty; walk before me, and be thou perfect. And I will make my covenant with thee, and will multiply thee exceedingly.'

Wow! I was gob-smacked. Bowled over. This was great stuff, streets ahead of anything Sharmah could have dreamt up. Do you see what Abram did there? In one short speech he positioned the event in time, which for humans seems to add credibility to any old tale; he established that something extraordinary had happened to him and only him, which immediately raised curiosity; he said a god appeared to him, which in itself is a conversation stopper. But it wasn't just any old god. He baited the hook with the drop-in *God of gods* then added some intrigue with the don't-speak-his-name thing. Moreover he used a word like covenant that no one understood, which meant they had to keep listening in the hope they'd figure it out and not look dumb by asking. Finally he ends with a hint of a promise of multiplication, which back then wasn't a mathematical function but a euphemism for sex – the time-honoured male crowd-pleaser.

Abe was utterly masterful. Picking him was like winning Lotto on a system seven.

For completeness I should add the rest of Abe's monologue, but as I never wrote it down (how could I?) I've included what someone claimed Abe had said, a few hundred years after the actual event. You'll note it's in English, a language neither Abe nor the scribe would ever hear since it was still a couple of thousand years into the future. The monologue is therefore my recollection of a translation of someone's distant memory of what someone else told them in a different language, so it might be a tad inaccurate.

Before you read it, I need to remind you about the two things I touched on earlier, because they both come out pretty clearly in his speech. Firstly he was the original land-grab developer with his eye on all the lands east of the Mediterranean Sea. And secondly he imagined himself to be an insatiable fornicator planning to populate those lands with his own offspring. With regard to the latter, I would also ask the more straight-laced readers to excuse his odd and persistent references to male reproductive equipment. For some reason Abe had a queer obsession with sperm (he called it seed but he wasn't talking about millet) and with foreskins, neither of which I ever really got to the bottom of.

Whatever conclusion you might be tempted to draw about Abe's sexual preference given his deep interest in male genitalia, I hasten to add he had a wife called Sarai, and a string of supposed offspring too, although whether any of them was actually his is still a moot point. He mightn't have been ninety-nine but he was no spring chicken either, and despite his plans to populate the Middle East single-handedly I don't recall a single night when he and young Sarai did the naughty.

In fact now I think about it, I'm not entirely convinced Abram liked Sarai very much. He certainly never liked her name because he was always trying to get her to change it Sarah – not a huge difference I admit; but it was a big deal to him for some reason. Actually Abram tended to mess with names a lot (as we'll see shortly) so why he didn't just call her Sarah and be done with it I'll never know. Indeed, most of the time I found it hard to fathom exactly what was going on inside his ego box, but he was good at spreading me about, and that was all that mattered. Anyway, here is the rest of what he said, every word of which he made up himself.

'I fell on my face, and God talked with me, saying, my covenant is with thee, and thou shalt be a father of many nations. Neither shall thy name any more be called Abram, but thy name shall be Abraham; for a father of many nations have I made thee. And I will make thee exceeding fruitful, and I will make nations of thee, and kings shall come out of thee. And I will establish my covenant between me and thee and thy seed after thee in their generations for an everlasting covenant, to be a God unto thee, and to thy seed after thee. And I will give unto thee and to thy seed after thee, the land wherein thou art a stranger, which is all the land of Canaan for an everlasting possession; and I will be their God. And God said unto me, thou shalt keep my covenant therefore, thou, and thy seed after thee in their generations. This is my covenant, which ye shall keep, between me and thee and thy seed after thee, every man child among you shall be circumcised. And God said unto me, as for Sarai thy wife, thou shalt not call her name Sarai, but Sarah shall her name be. And I will bless her, and give thee a son also of her, yea, I will bless her, and she shall be a mother of nations; kings of people shall be of her.'

When Abram finished speaking you could hear a pin drop. Pins were like roof nails back then so the hyperbole may not impress unless I remind you they were standing on soft desert sand at the time. But all acoustics aside, I think you get the point; nobody clapped, they just stared at him agog.

Initially I thought they were going to lynch him, until I poked around inside their adoring minds and realized we'd hit the jackpot. Whether it was his charismatic voice or the fact he'd promised more land and sex than they could eat, I can't honestly say; but the vast majority loved him.

Here was someone who really knew what he was talking about, because some new god – the God of all other gods no less – was speaking through him. Everyone was spellbound and virtually everyone bought it right away. There were a couple of sceptics in the audience who were a little slow to buy in, but as soon as they saw that everyone else was convinced, well they just went along for the ride, Sharmah style.

Then came question time.

At last.

At last.

At last.

'Pray Abram er... sorry Abraham,' asked a sycophant with the inevitable Dorothy Dix question. 'This one true God of whom you speak. Pray tell what is his name?'

The crowd hushed. Necks craned. Breaths held. Even I was poised. I don't have a heart, but if I did, and despite my being the instigator of Abe's ramblings in the first place, I'm sure it would have jack-hammered out of my chest. Why? Because after a million years give or take, I was about to get a name.

Speaking of names, just what possessed Abe to change his from Abram to Abraham is still one of the great mysteries of the Universe. There was no Deed Poll back then, so changing your name wasn't the pain in the neck it is today with bank accounts and passports and email addresses and all that, so he could have easily picked a nice two-dads name like Abramarmstrong-Jones or something equally grandiose. Slipping a few extra letters into Abram to make a nearly identical-sounding name like Abraham was a wasted opportunity, I thought. And why he picked *ham* to tack on the end of it I'll never know, but it has had a surprising knock-on effect over the years, which may have been part of the joke. From that moment on all his followers and descendents developed a fastidious and irrational horror of ham (all things porcine actually) and I often wonder if he was trying to tell everyone he liked ham and they just got it the wrong way around. We'll never know now; but I don't hear pigs complaining.

Anyway, back to my naming ceremony. I craned my figurative neck while my make-believe heart fibrillated. I tried to pretend I was cool about getting a name but to be honest I was so knotted up with anticipation I missed all the thought-chemicals whizzing around in Abe's head. I was therefore just as surprised as anyone when he said it.

'His name is YHWH,' he proclaimed, 'which thou shall not utter aloud, but only in silent prayer.'

'What?' said everyone including me. 'That's not a name. They're just letters.'

'I know. I know,' hushed Abe glancing up into the sky with fear as though there really was a God watching and listening. 'It's actually Yehoweh with the vowels taken out. So it sounds like Yowee. But you must not say it aloud.'

Clearly nomenclature wasn't Abe's long suit, and this was a silly way to go about naming a supreme being. In hindsight he probably should have just written down a name on a piece of parchment and handed it around so everyone could work out the pronunciation for themselves. But Abe was a talker not a writer.

Why he would pick such a soft and woosie name like YHWH for the God of gods still escapes me; but over the years I've developed a theory that might hold water. I now believe it was so no one *could* say it loudly, and if anyone got caught uttering it, they could just pretend they'd been clearing their throat.

'Yehoveh?' shouted Hymie Cohen who had only one good ear. 'We pronounce it Jehovah with a J on this side of the river. We can say Jehovah out loud, can't we?'

'No!' shouted Abe. 'You can't.'

'Eh?' said Hymie cupping his good ear to his neighbour. 'What'd he just call me?'

'You know I think he just called you a...'

Luckily Aron interrupted in the nick of time to save the huge punch-up that was surely brewing.

'P-p-pah!' he stuttered, still miffed at having missed out on the big job. 'J-J-Jeh-h-ovah's n-n-n-nothing special. There's a J-J-Jeh-h-ovah w-w-working d-d-down at the m-m-market p-p-place.'

Abe rolled his eyes and shook his head. Question time was clearly going to take much longer than he planned. But it was really his own fault. Apart from picking a silly name to begin with, he compounded the muddle by whispering the name in an old dialect of Hebrew, which through dry and wizen lips entangled in the mother of all beards, his Y's came out like J's.

'Not Jehovah! It's Jahweh.'

'Oh!' said Hymie. 'Itsjawie. I thought you said Jehovah. OK, got it. Itsjawie.'

'No, no! Not Itsjawie; just Jahweh.'

'Right, said Hymie clear at last. 'Joey it is then. Got it.'

'Oh for Pete's sake!' muttered Abraham. 'Yeah, yeah, whatever. You won't be saying it out loud anyway so I suppose it doesn't really…. Look, forget it. You don't need to know. Just remember saying it out loud is blasphemy. Blasphemers get stoned around here and I'm not talking weed. So no uttering!'

'Snow who?' said Hymie, confused again.

The clumsy banter carried on a bit longer, but I'd well and truly lost interest in the semantics. I've always been a bit anti-semantic anyway because it always ends with an antic.

But whatever Abe was trying to get at, Joey sounded like a pretty good name to me. I'd gone almost a million years without one so I wasn't letting this one go just because of some confusion with the local yargon.

If Muktuk was my mother, then surely Abraham had to be my father, for he had named me Joey.

And so it came to pass that my name was Joey. And so it was, and so it is, and so it shall be for all eternity. And I looked upon my name and saw that it was good.

And now I had serious work to do.

8

MILK AND HONEY AND HELICOPTERS

Now that I had a name, the first job on my to-do list was to make sure everyone remembered it. Abe was already convinced that there was only one God anyway, even though I'd just planted the idea in his head five minutes earlier, and since it was he who gave me the name Joey, there was little chance that he would forget it – his eventual dementia notwithstanding. But others would need reminding from time to time.

As to why Abe bought my story lock, stock and bible without question, I suspect it was because he was just as fed up as I was about which god did what and when, and he just wanted a simpler system to work under. Ambition did the rest, which is to say the Sharmah syndrome kicked in.

Abe, like every other human I've ever inhabited craved power over all other life forms including his own, and now that he had supernatural backing to realize that power, well... it was too good a deal to pass up. He grabbed it, owned it and pretty well hard-wired it into his future. Talk about lucky.

But whatever the reason Abe bought my story, we simultaneously came to the same obvious conclusion: we had to eradicate the competition. The multi-god stuff had to go.

This would be a feat incidentally, about as easy as arguing the sky was yellow, since multi-theism was deeply embedded in the population's psyche. Every king and queen on the planet had a personal stake in multi-theism since they themselves were self-proclaimed terrestrial members of that exclusive heavenly club.

It was one thing for a small group of followers to be swayed by Abe's charisma, but it was quite another to get whole nations to swallow it. Without radio, TV or Twitter to inject Abe's evangelism into doubting minds, nobody was going to ditch the multi-god concept just on a rumour, at least not without some serious groundwork being done first. But Abe was way ahead of me. Serious groundwork he did, and in doing so he gave me my first lesson in reverse psychology.

Quietly, without a lot of hoo-ha, Abe began slipping into his sermons the idea that his followers were the *chosen ones*, chosen by God that is for that most sought-after reward: yep, you guessed it, eternal salvation in the afterlife. *Heaven*, he called it, and quite a nice word it was too.

No matter what burden you had to carry in life, obedience to his words (my words actually) guaranteed you a great spot in heaven. And if that sounds familiar it's because it is. It was the same old Sharmah-promise adjusted for Hebrew. But Abe added a twist. Instead of encouraging everyone to go around bragging they were God's chosen ones, Abe actively discouraged his followers from mentioning it to anyone.

'Be humble of mind and purpose in His eyes,' he told them. 'Be not stiff-necked. Bow your heads to Him and speak not his name, for you and you alone are the chosen ones to know of His secret.'

Immediately I twigged onto why he had set up the *don't-utter-his-name* intrigue during his first performance. Nothing attracts interest more than a good secret. Nothing leaks worse than a good secret either. As soon as word got out that Abe knew the secret to a better life – a secret he was sharing only with chosen ones – a stream of malcontents were banging on his door demanding to convert; to deny all other gods; to worship only the capital G God and hence become one of the *ones*.

Who d'man? Abe d'man.

Please note here that I use the term malcontents in its literal sense and surely not to denigrate these poor souls. These particular malcontents had plenty to be malcontent about. Whilst I lack the requisite emotions to experience misery myself, I can certainly recognize it when I see it, and the vast majority of Abe's contemporaries were about as miserable as they come. Why? Well, back then the various kings of Ur wielded great power over everybody.

Sargon was dead by the time Abe came along, but he'd been succeeded by a steady stream of equally power crazed types with a *me King you worthless* approach to government – an approach which survives into the 21st century incidentally, with Saddam Hussein being its most recent practitioner. But back in Abe's day the practitioner was called King Ur-Nammu.

Ur-Nammu had great power, and as they say: *with great power comes great responsibility*. Actually, the unabridged version goes: *with great power comes great responsibility to crush everything and everyone you can lay your eyes on, to make sure you stay in power, maintain your self-esteem and keep a perpetual hard-on.* But the latter part hardly ever gets air-play because men don't like to admit that their penises are in charge of their brains, and will do anything to pretend otherwise. As you can see, nothing much had changed in male evolution since Raak made the jump.

Before you accuse me of judging men harshly, for women can certainly be nasty little critters when they set their minds to it, men are in a class of their own when it comes to people-crushing. Women don't even come close to the middle of that particular bell-curve; not by a long shot.

Over the millennia, the number of men I have inhabited who chose subjugating whole nations simply to manage their self-esteem far outweighs the number of women in that category by a factor of a good thousand. Indeed the true measure of male kingly power and esteem back then was the ability to crush subjects to the point where they were too weak and emaciated to fight back; which is about where Ur was in Abe's time.

As for why men are more prone to this sort of behaviour, it surely comes down to the waterbed-like sloshing of blood between brain and penis which, despite being the butt of many jokes (and vice versa), accounts for pretty-well everything bad that has ever happened anywhere.

Anyway, back to Abe's lot (lot with a small el, not his nephew Lot with a capital el who was a gambler and a bit of a loser) Abe's lot swarmed to him like ants to amber because they all wanted to get the heck out of Ur.

Famine was no stranger in these parts, and all Abe had to do was promise to lead them to a land of milk and honey, and they begged to follow him anywhere. The recent invention of agriculture had already denuded Ur of most of its lush foraging grounds, and thanks to a decades-long drought, Ur itself was quickly turning into a desert.

King Ur-Nammu had no objection to our leaving since he didn't much like the idea of upstart-Abe telling everyone there was a single God floating around in the air with more power than he had. And losing a couple hundred mouths to feed sounded like a good deal anyway, so he said good riddance to bad rubbish; and we all headed south for Canaan.

Once Abe took charge, he found he quite liked the idea of being the boss, especially as he was starting to believe his own propaganda – well, mine actually although he was convinced it was his. But without a police force to keep the peace, he knew he would need a powerful means of crowd control or the whole plan would go belly up before we reached the back gate. Here is what he did.

Up until now Abe had only ever talked about God being a benefactor. When they got to where they were going, there would be free milk and honey for all who believed –

so naturally everyone believed. After all, who joins a club with a stingy president? The time to read out the fine print was when there were plenty of fully paid-up members miles from alternate clubs. That was the time to quietly mention that this new God could also be vengeful; that if members didn't behave they'd get a lightning bolt up the ying-yang and a damn good smiting when they least expected it. And no health plan.

That is precisely what Abe did once the tribes had been wandering around the badlands of Canaan for a few months questioning the wisdom of following a self proclaimed centengenarian with no charts or compasses, save for a few stars in his cataracts.

Abe's approach to crowd control wasn't really any different to the one I'd been giving non-believers since Sharmah's day, *viz.* behave or suffer, but Abe's was on a grander scale given that he had gathered quite a flock about him measuring in the hundreds and multiplying. But the con only worked for a while. After three years of hunger and sore feet the novelty of the milk and honey thing really wore off.

The problem was that for all his imagination, ambition and oratory skill, Abe was a hopeless businessman, a shortcoming not shared by his modern descendents incidentally who now pretty much run everything. But back then Abe's entire strategy for claiming the Promised Land was to stand on a hill in someone else's backyard and shout, 'Hey! There's actually only one true God; he only talks to me, and he said I could have all this land. OK?'

Not surprisingly, existing incumbents were never swayed by this argument, and would tell Abe to bugger-off, frequently more emphatically than that. So understandably, after being run off five or six properties, Abe's followers started to get a bit toey. Mutiny was in the wind. Abe had to do something to show he was on the right track, and as usual he appealed to me for ideas.

Always one for testing people's limits, I suggested to Abe that he take his firstborn son up to the top of Mount Moriah and sacrifice him as a demonstration of his commitment to our plan. This put Abe in a bit of a quandary because he'd been a randy lad in his younger day and didn't really know who his firstborn son was. And even if he did, he'd be in his seventies by now.

Sarah's two current boys, Isaac and Ishmael were the best contenders, but since Abe was pushing a hundred by now and hadn't had sex with anyone in decades, these two so-called sons of his, barely in their teens, were a bit of a touchy subject around the campfire. Back in Ur, Sarah had told Abe that Isaac was one of those miracle children that to her very great surprise, simply popped out one night from between her legs.

At the time, Abe had been so focused on converting people to God-me that he just nodded and said congratulations. But when Ishmael popped out the following year Sarah knew she couldn't spin the same yarn, so she wove in a contrite twist.

'Another miracle,' she said. 'Isaac must have flushed out my plumbing. He has made it possible for us to have children again. If I'd known I would have fought harder to stop the goatherd hiding his salami inside me, I promise!'

If Abe had had some success with the Promised Land he might have bought her story, but as things were, he was feeling a tad grumpy and quite unloved, not to mention twice cuckolded. So, needless to say, he wasn't emotionally close to either boy.

He summoned Isaac because Ishmael was off milking goats or something (I forget now) and told him they were going up the mountain for a picnic. When they got near the top, Abe told Isaac to clear a nice flat rock, and set the table. But instead of spreading out sandwiches on the rock, Abe told Isaac to lie down on it, whereupon he pressed a bronze blade to Isaac's throat. At this point Isaac could see where things were going, and pushed Abe away. He'd only played along with the old codger at his mum's request anyway, but getting his throat cut hadn't been part of the deal.

'But Isaac,' Abe said. 'I have had a vision from Joey. I must sacrifice you as a measure of my devotion to him.'

'Tough tits, Pops,' said Isaac. 'I've still got some living to do, and some loving. There's this cute little daughter of a goatherd in the next camp that...'

'Oy vey,' exclaimed Abe. 'Sex, sex, sex. That's all you young bucks ever think about.'

'Well it was your idea to go forth and multiply!' countered Isaac. 'A bit hypocritical in my opinion since you've never kept your end up, so-to-speak. Mum says that's why Joey intervened and created me out of nothing.'

'Ah, that,' said Abe. 'Yes, well, I suppose I should have spoken to you about that, but right now I've got bigger problems. I told everyone that Joey expects me to sacrifice my firstborn. I crawled all the way up this bloody mountain to do it so I'm going to have to kill something before I climb down again.'

'Well surely Joey didn't mean me!' said Isaac thinking on his feet. 'He made me. I'm his miracle boy. You could say I'm *His* firstborn, not yours. And since Ishmael isn't yours either...'

'Ah, you know about that too, do you? Um, er you see your mother...'

'Forget it, Pops. Nobody cares. The point is you don't have a firstborn to sacrifice whichever way you look at it. So let's cut the crap, butcher a sheep, leave it for the wolves to eat instead of us, and let's get the hell off this friggin' mountain.'

I liked Isaac. He was a decent kid who put up with a lot of jeering from his friends about his hooked nose and who his real dad was, and that Ishmael didn't look even a bit like him, and so on; yet he never showed signs of needing therapy or anything. He just got on with life as well as any Bronze Age kid could.

I'd never had any problems with Ishmael either, who might have been next in line for the blade if Abe needed prodding next year. But on the way down the mountain, Isaac came up with a plausible reason why Abe wouldn't have to sacrifice anyone ever again: an angel had appeared in the nick of time and told him not to. Always the word-player, Isaac even convinced the old dodderer there was a modicum of truth in it.

'I was conceived by Joey, right?' he said.

'Well... yeah, we'll go with that.'

'That surely makes me part angel, doesn't it?'

'Mmm... I suppose you could....'

'Well, there you go, then. I'm the angel that intervened and told you not to make the sacrifice. You clearly demonstrated that you were willing. That's probably all Joey wanted anyway, so he sent a message to you through me, to stop you in the nick of time, and to say good job for obeying. Ta-da! You're off the hook.'

Back at camp, oddly, the crowd bought it, so that was the story for evermore – an angel intervened in the nick of time. Oy vey!

Five years later though, the Promised Land had proved so elusive that Abe's lack of navigational skill had become the only subject of discussion around the campfires. There was a distinct smell of mutiny wafting about in the smoke, so Abe's only viable option was to split up into tribes and search more efficiently.

We separated into seven tribes and we all headed off in different directions, each tribe looking for the Promised Land, and each promising to send a message back to the others when we found it.

Yeah right. This strategy might have worked if we'd been using long-range helicopters, but on foot it was doomed to failure. By the time anyone found land looking even remotely promised-like, Abe was dead, five generations had passed and everyone had forgotten what they were doing there in the first place. But even at split-up time, poor old Abraham had pretty much lost the plot; and to make matters worse the old coot accidentally stumbled into Egypt.

This was about as lucky as falling naked into a snake pit with only a good story to shoo away the snakes. Egyptians were into multi-theism in a big way and didn't take kindly to the idea of ditching all those gods on Abe's say-so. They had a god for absolutely everything, including (if you can believe it) cow dung, which in my opinion was surely a god beyond a joke; but they didn't think so.

Yes, Abe's novel concept (well mine actually) of a single God was so unpopular it was greeted with sharp spears, asp fangs and Nile drownings, all of which seriously discouraged theological debate for centuries. So the one-God concept spun its wheels all that time, which was the mere blink of an eye for someone like me who's been around for a thousand millennia but for Abraham it was just too long a wait – his dubious longevity notwithstanding – and he eventually gave up the ghost a broken man.

Now if you're sitting there thinking that this whole one-god exercise had been a complete waste of time, I can understand your reaching that conclusion. The world's population was tipping twenty million people by now with barely a thousand of them still liking the idea of there being only one God – especially after having trudged half way across the Middle East to try and prove it and failing so spectacularly. So you'd think that, over time, the God delusion would eventually get watered down to nothing – like homeopathic water.

But it's a funny thing about reductionism – some people really like it. Irrespective of veracity, the simpler the concept, the more likely some people will remember it and therefore believe it. More importantly, you need a lot less time to explain it to your kids, which means you can get a lot more work out of them. Even dear old Muktuk understood this back in the jungles of Chad.

She would just say, 'listen here kids, you're all going to die one day, so watch it!'

She didn't delve into the complexities of what death meant, or how many different ways there were to die, or any of that philosophical stuff. That would have just cluttered their sweet young gullible brains and occupied valuable space. No, she just kept it to that one short sentence – essentially inventing the principle of keeping things simple for the stupid.

So, far from being diluted, the descendents of Abe's followers actually flourished under the one-God secret because they weren't being distracted from the business of survival by having to teach and memorize four or five thousand god names to their kids, the way Egyptian parents were.

Just think about it: it takes the average kid about sixty repetitions to remember anything at all. At best, a god's name and what it was god of took about twenty seconds to recite out loud. Do the math and you'll see that working at it for six hours a day would take a whole year of valuable survival time. Then there's the revision and ritual and exams that go with it.

Meanwhile Jews would be out there learning about stock options and pork belly futures (they couldn't eat them but no one said anything about trading them). No wonder the Pharaohs eventually disappeared, and my lovely Jews survived. Indeed in the few hundred years since Abe died they'd survived so well that the Pharaoh began to get worried there were too many of them for comfort, so he decided to reduce numbers.

He'd heard that some mythical ancestor of the Jews called Abraham had been involved in a ritual of sacrifice of firstborn sons back in the days of yore, so he decided to take a leaf out of their history book. This had an unexpected and unfortunate consequence which I'll explain in a minute, but to appreciate the irony you first have to understand Pharaoh mentality.

The Pharaohs were a particularly strange lot – which for humans is saying something. Apart from having a seriously nasty opinion about everyone but themselves, they were utterly convinced they were actual gods temporarily residing on Earth, and were thus single-mindedly obsessed with returning to the afterlife. This was why the Pharaohs hated Jews so much. Jews doggedly adhered to a one-God policy, so how could a line of Pharaohs possibly argue they were all gods if there was only ever one? Pharaohs really hated that idea. It blocked the path to the afterlife, and they wanted their afterlife. It was all they lived for.

So with the afterlife dominating their future planning, each new Pharaoh would try to outdo his, or in Cleopatra's case her predecessors as to how much worldly stuff they could take to the afterlife to make sure they were as comfy as they could be when they arrived. From here you could draw a straight line back to Sharmah's burial cave, but flint knives and bearskins had given over to gold spears and naked concubines.

The Pharaohs' single-minded obsession with the afterlife incidentally was a direct result of having to learn about and satisfy the needs of too many gods here on Earth. It so dominated their thinking that it took over that part of the brain where normal people store common sense; and it clearly demonstrates the fundamental danger of pretending there are multi-gods – after a while that's all you can think about, and you don't notice what else is going on around you. The Egyptian tomb therefore turned into a kind of gravitational black hole into which everything of value including furniture, livestock, slaves and common sense got sucked.

Eventually, as resources began to dwindle because they were being buried faster than they were being produced, Pharaohs needed someone to blame. Jews were reproducing like rabbits, so Jews were the obvious target; and Pharaohs started thinking about how to cull them. This was the first time Jews were blamed for other peoples' mistakes, but it wouldn't be the last.

Meanwhile I had been busy looking for another Abe to reinvigorate my one-God version into an organised movement. The population had reached a tipping point to where I thought God-me might have a reasonable chance of expanding beyond the borders. But guys like Abe were few and far between, and it took ages to find one, especially using my alphabetical approach.

After nearly six hundred years I was up to the Ms and noticed a chap called Moses who looked like he might fill Abe's sandals. Moses had all the appropriate competencies: good talker, knew the Pharaoh culture, looked like Charlton Heston and all that, plus he had more than one idea how to get a Pharaoh's attention.

Moses was surely the first recorded double agent in history, albeit an unwitting one. Although he was raised an Egyptian in a Pharaoh household, he was actually the firstborn son of Jewish parents at a time when Jews weren't allowed to have firstborn sons. His mother had sent him as a baby down the Nile in baby-basket Sargon-style to avoid the chop. Meanwhile his sister had snuck along the bank keeping an eye on the basket as it drifted, until she reached a bend in the river where by chance Mrs. Pharaoh and her entourage happened to be picnicking. To attract attention to the basket Moses' sister threw some rocks at it, and the splashes did the trick.

By an amazing stoke of luck, Mrs. Pharaoh was in her clucky phase so she kept the little chap and raised him as her own, teaching him all about gods and what a powerful one her husband was, and how important pyramids were and so on. She even named him Moses after her husband, the Pharaoh Thutmose III. She told everyone the wee lad was Thutmose's, and the name stuck. See how easily some people get names! I had to wait nearly a million years for mine, and even then it got muddled up. Chemical patterns have to work really hard to gain recognition.

Anyway, by the time I spotted Moses as a likely Abe-successor, he was already fully competent and fully accepted into Pharaoh-world. He was as close to perfect as I could hope for.

So Moses grew up believing he was part of the Pharaoh line, and even expected to be a great leader one day. But eventually his hooked nose was a dead giveaway, and even he finally twigged that he had to be Jewish. Naturally he was conflicted about having roots in the underdog class while living like a king in the upperdog class, but he wisely kept his ancestry issues to himself because he knew his step-dad Thutmose was seriously anti Semitic.

I reminded Moses that despite his Jewish relatives being underdogs they were also a close-knit community outnumbering the Pharaoh class by about ten thousand to one. And numbers count for a lot.

'What is the secret of their close knitted-ness?' asked Moses.

'Only one God to satisfy,' I told him, 'and an invisible one at that – who didn't expect gold and slaves to accompany their owners into the afterlife. Heaven had all the wealth it needed,' I added.

Moses thought this was a pretty cool idea, so he tried to convince Thutmose that with so much valuable produce being wasted in pyramids on multi-gods, concentrating on just one God might actually help Egypt's ailing economy.

Apparently he didn't explain it right because Thutmose got outraged at the thought of lying all alone in a half-built pyramid with no one to keep him company. His enraged response was to evict the ungrateful Moses from the palace for trying to incite sedition, and to double his shift down at the construction site.

Because Moses was so grateful for his lavish upbringing, the guilt-ridden outcast thought the best thing he should do was knuckle down and work double time, and forget about my radical ideas. But I had other plans. I convinced him he could still be a great leader if he turned a bit awkward and make a stand for the little guy.

Well I must have touched a nerve because Moses eventually took me seriously and instigated a labour strike of genuinely biblical proportions right in the middle of a critical phase of Thutmose's pyramid project.

The project was already behind schedule because a once-in-a-hundred-year frog plague had interrupted supply lines down at the river. Worse still a locust plague was eating all the straw for the bricks, and was thus eating up all the float in the schedule. This put the entire project on the critical path, which is to say Thutmose would probably die before the tomb was ready – humiliating for any self respecting Pharaoh-god. So naturally when Thutmose saw his striking workforce sitting around eating his food and playing footy with his soldiers and chatting about promised lands he decided some serious motivation was necessary to bring Moses' mob back into line.

Since I was also inside the Pharaoh's head, I mentioned my old favourite of firstborn son eradications to get his workers' attention. It hadn't worked very well when Moses was a baby, but perhaps it might work this time. To Thutmose's credit he did try it, but it didn't work any better than the last two times I'd suggested it. I admit I can be a slow learner about some things.

But in my defence the reason it failed this time was that by now firstborns outnumbered soldiers by about three hundred to one, and since the workers knew the layout of the pyramid better than the soldiers did, there were a lot more places to hide. It was a disaster right from the start, and it humiliated Thutmose even more.

In a frenzy Thutmose raised the stakes to an all-born sons and daughters eradication program aimed at Jews and anyone who looked like one. That definitely got Moses' attention, and he finally saw the writing on the wall – in fact he wrote it. He put up a big sign announcing that he was quitting his job and leaving Egypt for good, and if anyone wanted to join him they were welcome, but the exodus wasn't going to be the ambling stroll that ancestor Abe had undertaken several hundred years earlier.

As it happened, 2.5 million people took him up on his offer, so stealth was out of the question. They packed up and took off out of Egypt as fast as their sandaled feet could take them, retracing Abe's steps more or less in reverse. The ensuing dust storm they created confused the Pharaoh into thinking they'd started work again down at the site, which gave them a useful head start. But after a spot inspection of the deserted worksite, the cavalry was hot on their heels.

Interestingly, Moses used the same milk-and-honey routine that Abe had used to motivate the crowd, but for some reason deliberately avoided talk of going forth and multiplying. Personally I didn't think it would work because my observation of mankind had been that sex was the underlying reason men did anything at all due to its beneficial effect on self-esteem; but Moses was adamant. Despite my strong recommendation that sex stay in the mix, he ignored me. Milk and honey were all that he promised, but he never said why. I simply assumed I'd underestimated the human craving for sweet, animal and insect exudations; but there was more to it than that.

On our way out of Egypt, Moses led us via the boggiest route he could find – across a very wide but shallow mudflat choked with tall reeds – and I started to wonder if I'd picked another loser. But as it turned out it was a stroke of brilliance. Boggy ground was certainly slow underfoot; but it was downright impossible under horseback. The cavalry got well and truly stuck in this muddy reed sea – which would later be confused with the Red Sea – and as a result we all got clean away without so much as a speared gluteus maximus. That's when I understood why Moses hadn't mentioned multiplication. The last thing we needed was a bunch of newborn sprogs slowing us down. Smart eh?

Along the way, Moses had similar problems to face as Abe had faced keeping the peace, but this time Moses had a population the size of upstate New York to manage. Luckily more people could read by then so all Moses had to do was chisel some rules and regulations onto flat rocks and have his lieutenants read them out every Saturday. That way no one could say they forgot it was against the law to covert his neighbour's ass, or his neighbour's wife's for that matter.

These Ten Commandments were my first introduction to the power of mass media, and I immediately recognized the potential for spreading me about; but I would have to wait three thousand years for Gutenberg to invent the printing press, and for Martin Luther to make good use of it. Until then I would have to be satisfied using imperfect salesmen like Sharmah, Abe and Moses and all the rest.

Now if you're a Bible reader you'll know that Moses had exactly the same success as Abraham in finding a Promised Land, and I want to state here and now, for the record, that I never promised either of them anything. Their grass-is-greener approach to crowd motivation was entirely their own creation, as was the inevitable disappointment that ensued.

I mention this because I want to make it clear that nothing is ever my fault. How could it be? I'm just a thought remember. People are free to choose how they use me, or not, as the case may be. Good, bad or indifferent it's all the same to me. All I can say for sure is that you're going to die one day. In my humble opinion the evidence is pretty compelling, but at the end of the day, whether or not you believe you are going to die one day is entirely a matter for you. And, whether you choose to make up stories to maintain a modicum of self-esteem while you're alive, in the face of clear but humiliating evidence that you can't prevent death; or even what happens after you die... well that is also entirely a matter for you.

Don't blame me for the trouble it causes.

9

BEWARE THE RIVER OF TRUST

I can already tell you think I'd been spending too much time getting my one-God version established, to the detriment of my multi-god versions. But one-God was just one experiment in a multitude of experiments I'd been conducting all over the world, and am still conducting today. My one-God version was simply a snazzy way of competing with my multi-god versions, to see which version would do better in the community of gullible minds. And this Supreme Being concept was just one subset of the overarching concept that everyone is going to die one day. It all stems from there.

If you were so disposed then, and you had enough time to do it, you could draw a family tree of all religions starting from the myriad that exist today, and work your way back to Sharmah's original gig. But what would you put below Sharmah, at the very base of the tree; at the tap-root, so-to-speak? Simply this: *You are going to die one day*. Everything else follows from knowing that; or more precisely everything else follows from me.

Remember my ambition was and still is to be inside everyone's brain, regardless of race, colour or creed, or species for that matter although I'm still no closer to cracking that particular nut than a quadriplegic squirrel is. The point is I didn't start out with the intention of becoming humankind's answer to a Supreme Being. That part came from your own internal greed mechanisms. I had very little to do with it.

I'm not criticising, by the way; greed is a great survival technique for individuals. And provided you can cope with everyone else's being greedy around you, you'll do pretty well as an individual. But if you plan to live in groups with neighbours and friends and all that, then variation is always going to motivate someone to be greedier than everyone else. You (assuming it's you) will want to be the boss, and bully less greedy people into becoming your slaves – or employees if you adopt a monetary system.

The problem is the more successful you become at this, the more you'll dominate, and the more distance you'll put between yourself and your peons. At first a few loyal henchmen will suffice to keep the hordes obeying your rules, but when you run out of loyal henchmen (as you will) you'll have to supplement your rules with imagination. You'll have to invent a vengeful spook who's watching from above, ready to strike down in the worst possible way. Then jargon will kick in, and sooner or later you'll call this spook a god.

This is all your doing, not mine. I simply want everyone to know they are going to die one day. What they choose to do with that bit of information is my playground (I need my fun too) but fundamentally it's up to each brain to choose its own path. My motivation is simple – it's about numbers. I want to be the most popular idea in the world.

Why do I want this, I hear you ask? Why not, you hear me reply. Does a thistle ask why it spreads so many feathery seeds across the glen? And when those tiny helicopters fall on fertile soil and grow into fertile thistles, does the original thistle protest that it's being too successful? If so, I haven't caught one saying it yet and I've been around a lot longer than you have.

Or does a salmon ask why should it lay millions of eggs when only a few might survive? No, it's hoping that all salmon egg eaters are on holiday, thereby allowing every egg to reach salmonhood. And if that fortuitous happenstance arose would Mommy Salmon be disappointed and ask her offspring to defer mating to reduce numbers? No of course not.

Our job – mine and yours, the salmon's and the thistle's – is to make more mes and yous, salmons and thistles respectively. Our job is to go forth and multiply; everything else is just show business.

In my own case I don't particularly care what people do for show business as long as they spread me about into more and more brains. If a one-God version appeals to more brains than a multi-god version (or a no-God version for that matter, but more on this later) then so be it – that's the version of me that spreads about the most. They're all still me; there is no other me.

Remember I've only popped up once – in Muktuk's brain. She spread me into the best survivors – your ancestors – so here I am in all my many forms. But we are all still me.

As far as I know, no one else has borne unto themselves a rival version of me. I'm inside almost everyone's head so I'm sure I'd have noticed. But even if a rival does pop up in the future, I'm not too worried because when you think about it, what would a rival version of me sound like? Presumably it would be something like: you're *not* going to die one day; or perhaps: you're going to die next Tuesday. Both would be pretty poor survival strategies in anyone's book, and surely accounts for why neither has caught on.

I should mention here that there *are* people who believe they are going to live forever, which isn't the quite same as believing they aren't going to die one day. I inhabit heaps of people who know they are going to die one day and simultaneously believe they are going to live forever. This apparent contradiction is actually a good survival strategy, since it motivates them to make long-term plans beyond the average life span, so they never die of boredom.

Where does this odd misconception come from? How can someone believe contradictory things at the same time without being or going insane? Well, without pre-empting a future chapter on what insanity really means, it is because of a pretty little chemical pattern that lives quite close to me, called Self Delusion.

She (you don't mind if I call her she, do you?) is a seductive little thing, and she gets into almost everything you do. I love watching her curvy voluptuous molecules caress your thoughts when you're looking at yourself in the mirror, or driving a car, or buying a Lotto ticket or engaged in public speaking.

She's right beside you convincing you that you're the best looking, best driving, soon-to-be rich, best public speaker known to man or woman – even though deep down you should know you're not likely to be any of those things. She lets contradictory ideas cohabit perfectly comfortably in the old brain box by exploiting pleasure chemicals in much the same way I do. She's also a big player in the game, and definitely a force to be reckoned with, but she doesn't share my ambition for world domination.

She's not an idea like I am; she's simply a chemical by-product of everybody's having too much imagination and being addicted to the pleasure of boosting self-esteem. Mostly she's just fun. She'll let you think you can easily fit into those size-five shoes whereas in reality your splayed meaty pads barely dent new snow. Or she'll delude you into thinking you look more handsome with a gold chain around your open necked shirt. And that's all good fun.

But sometimes she isn't fun; sometimes she'll convince you (for example) that you can drive a car and text your friend at the same time, or wade across a crocodile infested creek without being eaten. This is when she is at her most dangerous. People only engage in such self-evident foolishness because Madam Self Delusion has utterly convinced them that they are invincible, that their lives are mapped out forever; set in stone; destined to play out to a ripe old age far, far into the future; whereas in reality death is just one millisecond's inattention away. This is when people get a quick and final lesson in her power. She's a killer through and through. Don't ever forget it.

Personally I just love her. Why? Two reasons. One, she allows people to pretend their lives won't be over when they die. She has convinced most of my hosts that a ghostly replica of themselves will rise from their bodies and float on gossamer wings up to the afterlife. As to why people might love such an idea, and choose to believe it even though no one in the history of the universe has ever witnessed it, it's because she's given this self-delusory process the gorgeous name of Faith.

Faith is my favourite name, and I sometimes wish Abe had given it to me. With a name like Faith I could get people to like me in my basic form instead of resorting to deception and subterfuge.

Her deluding people into believing there's a nice place to go after death is a great help to me because let's face it, I'm a pretty unpleasant thought. No one enjoys thinking about me – that they are going to die one day – even though they might feel good about remembering it. The result is still pretty grim. But Madam Self Delusion comes to my rescue by pretending death is just a steppingstone to a better place; that all those nice things people have made up over the years, like Valhalla and Heaven and all that, are real, ready and waiting. I can't help but love her for that alone.

The second reason I love her is because she helps me creep into the corners of young minds so easily. Youngsters are particularly attuned to her siren-like call so kids will delude themselves about pretty much everything. You were a kid once; you know what I'm talking about: Santa Claus, tooth fairies, Easter Bunny and the like. But the greatest delusion children suffer is that they think everything their parents tell them is true. Better still, they will frequently believe what any grown-up person tells them, despite all the warnings about stranger-danger.

Working in tandem, Madam Self Delusion and I can boost kids' beliefs to dizzying heights. Together we can make any story seem positively enthralling, and set kids up for a lifetime of blind faith, even though what they read and hear are usually just strings of nice words sewn together with no supporting evidence at all. How else do you think Sharmah, Moses and the rest got everyone dancing to their tunes? How, for instance, can a land be made of milk and honey for goodness sake? What are the cows and bees supposed to eat? More milk and more honey? So where did it all come from in the first place? Sheesh! If listeners gave five seconds quiet thought to the words instead of being seduced by the music they'd quickly realize it was all a con. But they never do because Madam Self Delusion whispers softly into their willing ears that everything is so much easier when someone else does their thinking for them. I sometimes wonder why people go to all the trouble of growing brains at all, but thank Random they do, otherwise I'd be out of a job.

Speaking of jobs, my next big one popped up rather unexpectedly in 50 AD (as you measure dates) and afforded me a really big promotion. The promotion took me right to the top, and put me in charge of just about everyone and everything. But it's a promotion some of you won't want to accept.

As I mentioned already, Moses had no luck finding a Promised Land – by definition I suppose, since I never promised him one – and he eventually died a broken man. His failure disillusioned his followers in much the same way that Abe's followers were disillusioned when Abe died wondering why God had played such a cheap trick on him. And with disillusionment came the inevitable splinter groups demanding more and more outrageous requirements for reserving a room in heaven.

Splinter groups were a good thing for me because they provided more fertile ground to play in. If Moses' descendents had simply agreed they'd been conned, I'd have received a major set-back. I'd have lost all the one-God ground I'd made since Abraham, and I would have had to revert back to my multi-god version. While this wouldn't have been a disaster, it would have been disappointing because I'd been having a lot of fun with my one-God version.

Although my multi-god versions still flourished elsewhere (particularly in Rome), keeping the org chart up to date was quite exhausting; too much like hard work, and I didn't really favour that approach. As much as I hated to play favourites, I had to admit I had a soft spot for one-God me, so I wasn't ready to ditch it just yet. Moses' followers could so easily have thrown in the towel, but thank Random they didn't, because something wonderful was just around the corner. But it will take a while to explain.

You see, when my dear friend Madam Self Delusion stepped in to make Moses followers hold on tightly to what was apparently a lost cause, she was actually setting them up for the dooziest mass delusion trick of all time, and did the groundwork for my big promotion still to come. I'll tell you what her trick was in a moment, but let me first give a general example of her power.

Having watched the workings of human brains for a million years now, I can say with very great accuracy that whenever people realize they've been conned, a unique but fleeting moment of choice appears – a window of opportunity, you might say. People who realise they've been tricked are given a one-off chance to admit their mistake, to throw out the old ways, to start afresh and to take a better route, even if it means swallowing their pride, allowing their self-esteem to take a dent, and admitting they've been duped. The window of opportunity is open for a very short time, but while it is, people are in total control of their thoughts. It's one of those crossroads I hear them jabbering on about from time to time when absolute humility is required to ensure they take the right road.

But lucky for me this window has curtains. Madam Self Delusion will draw them closed as soon as she senses the slightest hesitation. Then as she pulls the cord, she'll distract with sensuous moves and reassuring baby talk.

You know what I'm talking about – that moment when you're drifting along on your raft of certainty. Your friends are with you, all perfectly assured that someone up front knows where you're going; and you're happy to float along with them, when suddenly you arrive at a fork in the river. The main part of the river is wide, comfy and familiar, but it bends in the wrong direction and you begin to doubt the skipper's motives. The other branch is narrow, unfamiliar and flows erratically. Deep down you know the narrow one is in the right direction but it looks like hard work; you'd have to carry the raft over rocks for a while then navigate all by yourself afterwards.

Primal Fear peeps out of his cave. You sense his presence. Worse still you feel the eyes of your friends glaring, frowning and admonishing you for daring to questioning the skipper's wisdom; so you look the other way, down the more familiar river. Primal fear slips back into his cave. You feel so much better. Better to feel better than to think for yourself.

But a few other rafts are also clumping at the fork. Do they sense what you sense? You look for the skipper. Where *is* that charismatic chap with the big boat? He's nowhere to be seen. You begin to wonder why you think of him as the skipper in the first place. He's really just a guy with a bigger boat, whose self-esteem feeds on the subservience of others. More doubt creeps in. You begin to wonder why you've been following him aimlessly down this river of trust.

People on the bank are waving their arms, shouting something about a big waterfall downstream – a dangerous waterfall. Even if you survive it, there's no coming back. Yet the river looks so smooth; can it be true? The moment has arrived. The window opens. You're on the cusp. You have to decide. Which way? Which way?

Then, bless her cotton socks, Madam Self Delusion whispers gently to help you decide.

'Still waters run deep', she reminds you.

You've heard it many times before. You still don't know what it means, or even if it is useful information, but it always sounds so wise; so comforting.

'But the people on the bank?' you protest. 'What about the waterfall?'

'Go with the flow,' she coos.

'Will someone show me what to do?' you ask.

'Hush my pretty, of course. Have faith.'

She helps you to remember: faith is good. You get nice promises when you're faithful, and nasty looks when you're not. Being faithful means never having to get nasty looks.

'But the waterfall?'

'Hush I say again my faithful one. Do you *see* any waterfall?'

'Well... no. But, what if...?

'Oh sceptical one. So many questions. So much doubt. Doubt is your enemy. I am your friend. Have I not brought you here safely and blissfully? Has your faith not served you well all the while?'

'Well... yes, I suppose.'

'You see? Faith provides. Worry not; believe in me.'

She's so knowing, so wise and convincing. Her warmth comforts you as you drift downstream, around the bend and away from the people on the bank. They shake their heads in despair and turn away. The window closes. We've won.

So what was her trick, and what was that *something wonderful* just around the corner in 50 AD?

Well, read on...

10

JESUS CHRIST! A SEVEN-CENTURY CYCLE

The seven-century cycle took me completely by surprise; yet if I'd been paying attention for the past million years, I could have easily predicted its coming. But for all those years I'd been under the misapprehension that humanity was randomly bumping along from one mess to the next without rhyme, reason or pattern. Now I realize that is not the case.

I suppose I had to go through a few cycles of boom and bust before noticing a pattern existed at all, but now that I look back to the time of Sharmah and project forward to the present day I can see the pattern so clearly.

At times whole nations would be utterly enthralled with my ideas irrespective of which particular god-form I was in, and would go to great lengths to insist other nations be equally enthralled using various strategies like invasion, torture and genocide to make their point.

Yet at other times my popularity would dwindle and I would find myself inside heads that had become bored with the *status quo;* heads that wanted to change things. If I'd kept records I'd have noticed a pattern – a seven hundred year cycle would have jumped off the page.

Looking back it's obvious that roughly every seven hundred years give or take a hundred; a small percentage of my hosts would come to a fork in their particular river of trust, and begin to doubt everything their elders had been telling them. Each time without fail, the doubters would have a short fight with the main group – sometimes quite a nasty one – then they would split off and start a new version of me, imposing all sorts of new beliefs and rules onto willing followers. For my part it was easy enough to convince such rebels that they were right and the mainstream was wrong, because that's exactly what they wanted to hear. But I'd never realised I could have predicted it.

With the benefit of hindsight the seven hundred year cycle stands out like a Burka at a bar Mitzvah, and surely accounts for why there are so many versions of me. But until 50 AD I'd never done the maths. Once I did, the evidence was compelling.

You can do it too. Count forward from the Hindus, the Sumerians, the Egyptians, to Abraham, the Buddhists and to Moses, and you'll see it plain as day: seven hundred years, give or take a bit.

Why seven hundred? I'm really not sure, but it probably has something to do with each generation becoming incrementally annoyed at their elders' ways of doing things. Perhaps it takes ten lifetimes to work up the courage to rebel. Who knows? Indeed, who cares? What matters is that I've discovered a way of anticipating the next cycle.

This discovery struck me in the year 50 AD in Palestine – the original one, not the mini version you know today. There was this Turk called Saul who was heading back to Damascus from a business trip in Jerusalem. He was feeling furious about something he'd seen back in Jerusalem, when suddenly he stopped in the middle of the road and had an epiphany.

The Romans, as you know, were a terrific race, and they made terrific roads, so Saul's epiphany had no effect on the road itself, but it was destined to have a profound effect on the future of the world, including yours.

It all started because he'd been thinking about a bunch of his Jewish mates back in Jerusalem, who had been preaching all sorts of stories that weren't in any scriptures he'd ever read.

This bothered Saul greatly because he was a devout Jew if ever there was one, and he fancied he knew his scriptures forwards, backwards and inside out. At the time, I hadn't been paying much attention because to be perfectly honest I'd been feeling a bit dejected. Here's why.

Up until Saul's epiphany (which I'll explain shortly) nothing was much fun anymore. The Romans, who essentially ran Europe and the Middle East, had a strict, multi-god policy and they insisted everybody worship my manifold versions or die. So understandably my one-God version took a back seat. Jews still loved the idea of one-God me but they were outnumbered by a gazillion to one, so they kept quiet and laid low, becoming seriously introverted and introspective in the process.

Far from spreading me around, Jews had developed a closed culture, aggressively shunning new recruits unless the recruits were blood relatives. Unless you were a Jew, you couldn't become a Jew. Weird eh?

Well, as I'm sure you know, if you only allow blood relatives to join a club, sooner or later you end up marrying a sibling and having offspring with more off than spring. Even if they survive they'll have overbites and a tendency to drool, and really bad eyesight. This is precisely what had been happening to Moses' descendents.

The dangers of a shrinking gene pool weren't lost on Saul who fancied himself as custodian of all things Jewish, but he was two thousand years short of cracking the double helix so he never really expected to be able to do anything about it. Then he started thinking, which is when I pricked up my imaginary ears. This was his epiphany.

'Those guys might actually be onto something,' he said to his donkey.

I know it doesn't sound much, but neither did I when I first popped into Muktuk's head. The lesson here is: never under estimate an epiphany. You never know where it might take you.

Those guys incidentally, to whom Saul referred, were called James and Simon – two Jews that ran a renegade synagogue back in Jerusalem. Saul didn't like James very much because he was always bragging about having a supernatural brother; but Saul and Simon were reasonably good mates at the time. It wasn't to last.

When Saul saw what Simon was up to, viz. preaching that everybody should be treating everybody else equally, and turning the other cheek, and pretending that he'd worked for the son of God for three years, and things like that, well Saul just did his block. In his anger he did something unforgivable even for biblical times. He did a spot-audit of Simon's congregation and to his horror discovered it was seriously lacking in the circumcision department.

Although I never actually caught him lifting anyone's frock to check, he was absolutely convinced that Simon had dropped the snip-snip rule of entry into the synagogue, and was letting any old anybody in to hear about what the son of God was up to.

This wasn't the first time I'd heard I had a son by the way, but it was the first time I realized that Saul had inherited Abe's fascination with male genitalia.

I say now of Saul's odd behaviour: I think he was a manic-depressive. Certainly his highs and lows matched Everest and the Grand Canyon perfectly; and there was no telling when he would flip from one extreme to the other. In fact the plethora of intact foreskins at Temple got him so worked up that I thought he was going to have a coronary. But worse was to come.

When Saul found out that Simon had also relaxed diet rules on eating leavened bread and rare meat and shellfish and so on, he got so enraged that he had a knock down, drag 'em out with Simon in front of the whole congregation, ending the friendship there and then.

By the way if you're wondering? No, I wasn't offended by Simon's pretending I had a son. Quite a few Moses wannabe successors had, in the past, claimed that I'd started a family and that I used my sons to do heavenly work on my behalf down here on Earth. But without living proof the idea never really caught on. I assumed this latest story about my being a single parent would peter out too, but Saul decided to feel furious about it and change everything.

All the way home Saul fumed about Simon's departure from orthodox teachings, when suddenly, during his epiphany he had a mild stroke that lasted a few minutes. It wasn't anything as dramatic as Sharmah's epileptic fit but it was just as far reaching.

When Saul recovered, it dawned on him that he was being handed the opportunity of a lifetime. If he played his cards right, he could solve the gene pool problem *and* set himself up as the head of a new and better Jewry. Better still, he would be able to give the smart-ass Simon the comeuppance he so richly deserved.

Now I was interested.

When we got back to Damascus we sat down and started writing. Saul's eyesight was still a bit dodgy from the stroke so he told his neighbours he'd been blinded by an insight from God (I thought it was nice he attributed it to me) and asked them all to leave him alone until he felt better. Then we got down to some serious writing.

During the next few weeks, sitting in a nice quiet room overlooking Damascus rooftops, we came up with some really good stuff: seven essays that knitted past events and present day wishes into some ripping yarns we called Romans, First Corinthians, Second Corinthians, First Thessalonians, Galatians, Philippians, and Philemon.

These were great stories about how humble, generous, decent people would one-day take over the world from the bastards who currently ran it; stories that would seriously appeal to the downtrodden. We chose the downtrodden for our audience because there were so many more of them than the up-trodden. And numbers are everything when you want revolution.

I have to say that despite his fits of mania and despair, or perhaps because of them, Saul was one of the smartest guys I've ever lived in. Instead of writing his seven essays as dissertations, or as background rules for his new religion, he wrote them as letters. Why? Because everyone knows that letters aren't fiction; they're true; right?

You don't write letters to your friends to entertain them with lies; you write them to describe things that actually happened to you. This put Saul ahead of the game even before he mailed them, because he didn't have to back up his writing with a whole lot of tedious bibliography, or have impertinent editors question this fact or that. These were letters; of course they were true.

Now when you write a letter, you write it to someone you know, right? Not Saul. Saul's genius was to write his letters to nobody – to people that didn't exist – but he sent them to people who did exist, so that they might open them, read them and then talk about them.

Back then people loved opening other people's mail as much as they do now, so Saul knew that whoever received a letter would surely open it, read it and be bowled over by its contents. Once they realised the letters were full of heretical stuff, they wouldn't want one sitting on their hard-drive, or tucked away in a teapot or anything like that, so they would pass it on to someone else and say, 'Guess what turned up in my letterbox? It must be for the previous owners. Want to read it?'

To make sure there were no returns-to-sender, he signed them as someone called Paul instead of Saul, and left off his return address so people couldn't send them back even if they wanted to. All people could do was pass them on to someone else. And since the letters' contents were literary dynamite, they were bound to attract an instant cult following.

As to why Saul chose the similar sounding name of Paul as his *nom de plume*, it wasn't because he shared Abram's lack of imagination in nomenclature. It was because there was always a slim chance that the forgery police would catch up to him and accuse him of signing someone else's name. If that happened, his plan was to say it was a mere slip of the pen, and he really meant Saul, not Paul. But the cops never caught him, so he ended up using either name when it suited him.

Anyway, the gossip generated by the letters swelled like a rock star's head, growing larger and larger until whole communities were talking. What a great way to start a new religion – by pretending it already existed. You see, Saul didn't write to people asking them to start a new religion; he wrote to them as though the religion had already been flourishing for years, invoking the usual *why wasn't I told* indignation that people love to have. The letters read like discussion points for existing believers to debate, and which had merely gone astray in the post. It was the scam of all scams and it worked a treat.

Now I can finally reveal to you the *something wonderful* that I teased you with earlier. It came about because Saul didn't set himself up as the head of his new church – he stepped aside for someone else. None of my protégé's throughout history had ever done that. To a man, they had all set themselves up as my earthly rep, claiming that I resided in the afterlife or in Heaven or Valhalla or wherever, while they resided on Earth to enforce the rules and reap the Earthly benefits Sharmah-style. It was standard operating procedure, and I expected Saul would follow suit. But Saul took a different slant.

Saul plagiarised one of Simon's ideas just to sock it to him, and said that the head of this new religion had walked among them years ago as a sort of human superhero, for whom performing miracles was daily fare. Moreover this superhero was the actual son of God no less – which is to say, he was my son.

I'd become a daddy, albeit an imaginary one, but that's probably as good as it gets for a chemical pattern. How wonderful was that? Saul had turned the other cheek so-to-speak and put my son in charge. Talk about practicing what you preach. He was a model for you all.

Saul originally named my boy Yahweh Jr. but quickly changed his mind because stoning was still the favoured method for discouraging Yahweh-utterers. So he chose a slight variant – similar enough to be obvious to everyone that he was still talking about the son of God but different enough to avoid being stoned to pulp for saying it. Yehovah and Yoshua were pretty close approximations but still had a hint of stoneability about them, especially if slurred through an overbite (see earlier). So he settled for a short, succinct Yeshu. But since he was a Greek-speaking Turk making up a Hebrew name, the J's and Y's got muddled again and it often sounded like Jesu.

Whether it was just dumb luck, or whether it was because Saul was an expert in the Talmud, it occurred to him that he'd already read about a Yeshu who had existed about 150 years earlier, around 100 BC by your calendar, although by now you'll be wondering why there's a BC and AD at all. And this particular Yeshu also had a rebellious nature, just like Saul.

According to what Saul had read, Yeshu was the illegitimate son of a Jewish girl called Miriam who had been betrothed to a carpenter called, coincidentally, Yoshuah, though people tended to pronounce it as Yoseph or more frequently Joseph, to avoid the stones.

Back then betrothal was a euphemism for engaged but not yet bonking. I don't remember Miriam all that well, but I do recall that for months and months the hormonal darling had been feeling trapped in the no-fun zone between furtive looks across the in-laws' dinner table and the nightly pounding she yearned for after marriage. But before the big night arrived, she bent over once too often in the vineyard to pick up a load of grapes, and a Greco-Roman soldier called Pandeira caught sight of her hitched-up skirt, and decided to dispense a load of his own.

A sucker for uniforms, Miriam succumbed to Pandeira's charms and got knocked up good and improper. Nine months later Miriam begat baby Yeshu.

As you can imagine, Miriam's dad wasn't too pleased when he found out his daughter was in the family way prematurely, and threatened to stone poor Yoseph for dispensing the premature ejaculate. But when Miriam did the math for her dad it was clear that her betrothed had been away that month delivering furniture, so it couldn't have been him. But neither could she bear the shame of admitting she'd opened up for a Roman, so she absolutely insisted she was still a virgin and that little Yeshu had to be a miracle baby.

This slow-learner of an excuse had been handed down from mother to daughter since Sarah's day as a last resort for unexplained pregnancies to dim-witted husbands, and I have to say it hardly ever worked. But a father was more likely to defend such a story to deflect attention away from the only other plausible explanation that he'd done the dirty himself, since the occasional father-daughter indiscretion wasn't unheard of among the hillbillies of Galilee. So both Miriam and her father stuck to their guns to avoid being stoned to death for incest.

But dad was no dill, and certainly didn't want another mouth to feed, so he expertly controlled the story by buying-off the cuckolded Yoseph's pride with a little gold, frankincense and myrrh, the result being that Miriam and Yoseph brought up little Yeshu as a full blood son.

This kind of family intrigue was actually pretty small beer for the times, because something like it would be happening on a monthly basis in one village or another, so you might wonder why little Yeshu's name made it into the Talmud at all. It wasn't because of his illegitimacy; it was because he caused so much strife when he grew up.

Yeshu had Sharmah-like qualities including the gift of the gab, good ideas, a charismatic voice and a mostly peaceful disposition and all that, but every now and again he would get frustrated at his fellow man and throw a tantrum, often at the worse possible time and place. His ultimate undoing was turning up at market time interrupting trade with speeches about how shitty life can be, and how I had told him that if everyone loved their needy neighbours and gave them food and alms and surplus wealth, then life would be so much better for everyone.

He himself was a needy neighbour so his speeches were driven more by survival than altruism, but he spoke nicely and managed to make enough friends that he got to the age of thirty-three living on handouts. But his biggest failing was making a promise he couldn't keep – a promise that directly competed with the prevailing Jewish power base. He told people that his way to Heaven was the only way to Heaven. If people practiced what he preached, then the Pearly Gates would definitely open up for them to a land of milk and honey, because his father, i.e. yours truly, was the gatekeeper. Sound familiar? That was just me again having a little fun.

But as much as I enjoyed it, it really annoyed the locals. Why? You see by this time we were well into the Iron Age. People had smartened up a bit, and everyone was just that little bit harder to convince. The stories of Abraham and Moses were too well known, so a milk and honey Promised Land spiel was never going to wash. Yeshu therefore didn't attract a huge following, but he nevertheless managed to annoy enough orthodox Jewish leaders to prompt them to complain to the local mayor – a Roman Centurion, no less.

Always favouring a violent solution to a diplomatic problem, the Centurion decreed that the townsfolk were perfectly within their rights to stone Yeshu half to death for disturbing the peace; which they did.

I was there of course (I'm everywhere) and when Yeshu was half dead I reminded him that he was going to die one day and this was probably the day. This time I got it right because the Centurion saw in the half dead lad the makings of a habitual repeat offender, so he hung Yeshu upside down from a tree to make him whole dead.

Both Saul and I agreed that the 150-year-old story of Yeshu would make an excellent foundation for a new religion, because it was just old enough to be beyond living memory, but just recent enough to still be relevant. To pull it forward to a more respectable time – so people could pretend they really could remember it – we set about writing accounts of messiah Yeshu's life in more detail to give the impression they'd happened just a little while ago.

We simply called those accounts *good news stories*, but given the lack of language quality control back then, and given people's ongoing love-affair with jargon, the phrase later got mashed up into *good spiels,* and later became know as gospels.

Saul made up the details himself, and deliberately kept the theme consistent across all versions but he wrote each version in a slightly different style to imply they'd been written by different authors. That way, sceptics were more likely to conclude the documents were factual and merely subject to the excusable memory imperfections of different contemporaries.

As I recall, Saul wrote twelve gospels, but only six or seven of them have survived the ravages of time. Many hundreds of years after Saul penned them they were (oddly) given men's names like Mark, Matthew, Luke, Andrew and Thomas to help various men who needed a self-esteem boost at the time, but I know Saul didn't write the one that was called John, because Saul was dead when it was written, which is why it is so different from the others.

Saul, ever the inspired nomenclaturist (not) decided he'd call his religion *New Judaism.* Knowing people the way I did, I tried to tell him the name would never stick, but sometimes you have to let people learn the hard way.

Meanwhile, to complicate things, back in Jerusalem, Simon was sticking to his guns about a more recent messiah called *the anointed one* who had since risen to Heaven. There's nothing like competition to get the inventive juices flowing.

Messiahs were actually pretty common during this era because a thousand years earlier, while Abe's lot were being persecuted, Abe and I made up a story about various saviours and messiahs who would appear in about a thousand years to set everything right again. Stories like that gave people something to hope for, but I never imagined they would actually last a whole millennium. Well, last they did and wannabe messiahs have made a nice living out of them along the way. The phenomenon continues to this day.

So, annoyed with Simon that he was competing in the messiah market, Saul casually dropped into one of his sermons that any rabbi worth his salt would surely know that the particular *anointed one* that Simon was taking about was obviously Yeshu, or Jesu if that pronunciation was easier. And if anyone needed written proof, the Talmud was simply brimming with it.

Saul's followers began embracing New Judaism whole heartedly, which momentarily threw Simon off guard, and Simon could have easily lost his credibility altogether. But then he did a couple of things that floored Saul forever.

The first thing he did was to change his name from Simon to Peter, to throw Saul off the track. Again with the name changes; no wonder your historians have trouble working out who did what and when. Anyway, Simon Peter, whom I'll call Peter from now on so please try to keep up, very cleverly reminded his followers that any Greek-speaking Turk like Paul, alias Saul, ought to know that *anointed one* was simply a Greek expression that didn't translate directly into Hebrew, and that the closest Greek word for *anointed one* was *Khristos*, and certainly not *Yeshu*.

A name war ensued for a few of months because no one wanted to back down, but eventually the conciliatory Peter proposed to Paul that they split the difference and agree their messiah be known as Jesu Khristos. I thought it was an excellent compromise; but Saul was as stubborn as tuberculosis and chose to disagree, at which point he made the strategic blunder of his life.

Instead of staying in Jerusalem to wear Peter down with superior intellect, Saul, who was by now overtly calling himself Paul, spat the dummy and headed north to Greece and later to Asia Minor to push his *New Judaism* gospels into more willing minds. I was there to help of course, reminding one and all of the awful ways they could die if they didn't tune in to Paul's wavelength, and I must say we did a damned fine job converting thousands to his new way of thinking, and convincing them I had a son, etc. But sadly for Paul he didn't get the recognition he deserved because nobody today has ever heard of *New Judaism*.

Peter, on the other hand stayed home in Jerusalem where he became more and more popular, not because he was any better at mind games than Paul – since I was working equally hard for both of them – but because Peter's version went by the catchy name of Khristianity. And as I keep telling you, names count for more than you'd think.

If you've been hoping for a happy ending to the Peter-Paul contest then the following will surely disappoint. Remember I've been telling the story from one side only – the Jews' side. There was also another side – the Romans' side.

To Romans, Christian and terrorist meant the same thing, the way Muslim and terrorist do today (more on this later). But back then in an empire where looking sideways at a Roman citizen was tantamount to treason, running around preaching that Nero was a false god was never going to end well.

Paul lost his head because of it (literally) which is surely the reason he was never considered to be the head of a church of anything. I mean how embarrassing would that be, worshiping a headless statue? But at least his death was quick and painless.

Peter on the other hand died in extreme agony but he retained ownership of his head during the entire process and thus stood a better chance of being the first Bishop of Rome, so I suppose it all balanced out in the end.

As for how Peter died, he finally got around to reading the Talmud, and in particular the part about Yeshu's life and death. He figured if stoning and hanging was a good enough end for the messiah it was good enough for him. He asked Nero to dispatch him the same way, but Nero said that was just plain barbaric in a civilized culture like Rome's, so he crucified him upside down instead.

Incidentally if any Christians reading this are feeling a bit duped (or annoyed) by my revelations, I don't blame you. Some seriously good brainwashers have been working on you since childhood with the Christmas story and Easter and walking on water and all that, so it's not really your fault. Don't beat yourselves up over it. Great wisdom comes after ten thousand mistakes, and this was one just one of them. Besides, walking on water is nothing special. Eskimos do it all the time.

But despite your distaste at what you've just read, consider that this may be your fork in the river. Take a moment to clear some clutter. Where did you get the idea it was all true anyway? From Mom or Pop perhaps? If so, where did they get it? Where did anyone get it? Think about that for a while, and after you've discovered the trick, think about where you go from here.

Where you choose to go is up to you, as it always should have been, but this time make sure it's your decision and not someone else's. Personally I don't mind where you go, as long as you remember you are going to die one day. That's all I'm here to tell you for certain.

And if you're a nice person suddenly moved to question your Christian paradigm, you don't have to abandon being nice. Niceness was already in you. There were plenty of nice people around before I invented Khristianity. One didn't follow from the other. Ditto for nasty, by the way.

Either way the blind-faith thing might be a tad conflicting at church so a bit of unbiased research on your part could boost your confidence. There are plenty of unbiased historians from that era to read up on – Pliny the Elder, Pliny the Younger, and Josephus Seneca to name three. And the life and troubles of people like Emperor Tiberius and Nero are well documented too. All the usual suspects are there in black and parchment. Even the name Pontius Pilate shows up on coins and chiselled inscriptions from time to time, but sadly no Jesus, Jesu, Iesus, Iesu, Yesus or Yesu has made any mark in history except the one I mentioned earlier.

If the Jesus you've been told about really did exist, I certainly wasn't in him. Perhaps he refused to believe he was going to die one day and wouldn't let me in. That could explain it, and certainly gives Madam Self Delusion a curtain-hold if you can't handle what I'm saying. But I've been inside almost every head before and since, and no one ever mentioned a Jesu-like name with reverence till Saul came along twenty years after the supposed crucifixion, when we made Him, and it, up. Still, it's not hard to see how the Talmud's Yeshu ended up as the Bible's Jesus after all this time, especially after the clever name tricks people play. So give yourself a break.

And if you're still annoyed at me for making you think for yourself, one piece of advice I would offer is the following. Next time you hear someone say something that you really, really, really want to believe, remember this: the nicer the voice, the more likely they're trying to trick you. Real Estate agents and car sellers are the benchmark here. As a minimum ask someone you don't like to repeat the words and see if they still make sense; or ask someone with a stutter to tell you over the phone. Then you can decide if it's really the words that are swaying you, or just the music.

So if Saul's and Peter's followers petered out under Roman oppression, what did this story have to do with the seven hundred year cycle? Well, they didn't all peter out. Like Moses' leftovers, a few hung on to their belief in one-God me but kept it to themselves. Meanwhile the current rulers of the day – the Romans – were making the same old mistakes that all previous rulers had made. They were getting fatter and fatter on excessive taxation, and lazier and lazier on a glut of slaves, while all the while annoying more and more people than they realized. Mentally the Romans were as hard as nails, having risen to the top using overwhelming, brute force. That's what iron does for you. Weapons were how they controlled things; they knew their weapons inside and out, and were constantly on the lookout for people who might have better weapons with rebellion on their minds. But the Romans were looking the wrong way. If they'd studied even a modicum of history they'd have known that rebellion never starts with swords – it starts with ink.

Saul's/Paul's letters were like slow ticking clocks on a nuclear time bomb. The clocks took about three hundred years to go click, but when they did, all Hell broke loose – literally, as it happens, since Christians invented the place – and the fallout from that explosion spread all over the Middle East and Europe and eventually made it to the Americas, spawning my largest crop of hosts in human history. But first the bomb had to go off, which it did – in Rome.

Here is how that happened.

When the Romans buried Peter they put a huge rock on his grave just in case the resurrection myth about souls rising to heaven might be true. This was a massive strategic error on Nero's part.

The stone marked Peter's grave, and nothing creates a shrine like a marked grave. If the Romans had fed him to the lions, things would surely be a whole lot different today because lion poo doesn't keep, and certainly doesn't inspire close worship. But they didn't; they marked his grave with a stone, so the memory of Peter lived on, biding it's time.

Peter had been my best carrier to date, but he certainly wasn't coming back anytime soon. With him gone, and since I can't predict the future any better than you can, I decided to archive the one-God program again and concentrate on the multi god version for a while.

I was already spreading brilliantly as the multi-god version, so it made little sense to keep the one-God strain active until a worthy carrier came along. The Romans, the Hindus, the Mongols, and the many tribes of the Americas, north and south were pumping out gods on conveyor belts; and with the Romans happy to use Christians as Coliseum cat food, it seemed inevitable that capital G God would die too.

Then in about 313 AD something utterly unexpected happened. Around this time, Roman emperors were at their all-time-warring worst, and the current one known as Emperor Caesar Flavius Valerius Aurelius Constantinus Augustus, sometimes known simply as Constantine was up there with the worst of them.

For some reason he was one of those blokes that nobody seemed to like, even though he was actually no worse than many of his predecessors. I thought he was all right, but his family really hated him because he had a tendency to kill his brothers and cousins the minute they showed any ambition for taking over his emperorship; so I could see their point.

While Constantine was on yet another campaign of the time-honoured European pastime of fighting Germans, the members of his family whom he hadn't killed yet plotted to take over the empire. Constantine heard about this and rushed back to Rome as quickly as twenty thousand men can rush, hacking his way through various enemy armies along the way to stay in shape. But getting back into Rome would be a different matter; Rome wasn't just built like a fortress, it was a fortress. And since Constantine had foolishly left very few friends behind to let him in, he found himself appealing to lesser enemies for support. One such lot was Rome's many underground Christians whom Constantine knew lived like rats in the sewers, but with whom he had no quarrel because they were inherently passive.

Affluent Jews were allowed to keep Christians as slaves, but these same Christians harboured a long-running grudge against Jews because they hadn't read the Talmud either and mistakenly believed that Jews had killed the Jesus that Saul and I had invented three hundred years earlier. Yes, Christians were passive, but they sure knew how to carry a grudge, even a mythical one.

Romans also kept Christians as slaves, but they let them eat better food and have nicer beds and a bit of furniture and so on, and by now were turning a blind eye to the one-God story that pervaded Christian thinking, so as a rule Christians hated the Romans of the time quite a bit less than they hated Jews.

When Constantine arrived at Rome's gates he was prepared to sack the city if that's what it took, but to show he had no quarrel with Christians, the politically brilliant fellow made his army wear Christian symbols on their tunics and shields in the hope that Christians would get the message that he wasn't targeting them.

Well, talk about lucky! Not only did the Christians understand Constantine's message, they decided to help him by staging a go-slow strike of Moses' proportions. And since Christians did all the work around town anyway, a strike would bring Rome to a complete standstill – a tradition that latter-day tourists will attest continues to the present day when Italian Unions get the same idea into their heads.

But back then all it took was a disgruntled gatekeeper. He'd been trying for months to get the maintenance department to fix a dodgy gate latch, and after submitting requisition after requisition and being ignored, he finally had enough. He walked off the job and headed straight to the nearest tavern, leaving the gate unlatched and unguarded. At the bar he bragged about his bravado to one of Constantine's spies masquerading as a wealthy drunk. The spy shouted a few more pints then slipped out the gate and gave Constantine the good news.

That night Constantine and five thousand troops walked into the city virtually unopposed and retook Rome with no gratuitous bloodshed save that of his last remaining relatives with emperorship on their minds.

With Rome now regained in such a weird and unexpected way – with the help of Christian slaves no less – superstition got the better of Constantine and he converted to Christianity, lock, stock and Crucifix; at which point the ticking nuclear time bomb went off.

Suddenly all over Rome – not just in the city but the entire Empire from Hadrian's Wall to the Dardanelles – it was fashionable to be a Christian. Everybody who was anybody was questioning the wisdom of having hundreds of gods when just one had done such a spectacular job of winning back the city.

Naturally I immediately re-booted the capital G program and started running it in every head in the world, and in less than a year the Roman Empire was mine. From a tiny diminishing point of near-extinction, my favourite version was suddenly the dominant view, and I've never looked back.

There were minor ripples along the way of course, but nothing I couldn't handle, and I even took advantage of one of them. It came just twelve years later in 325 AD when Constantine's bishops were getting uppity about who knew more about God and Heaven and all that. I found it mildly amusing of course, since I'd made it up anyway, but I let them play.

The question that troubled them the most was where did Jesus fit into God's family? God was a god – well *the* god obviously, and clearly Jesus was a god because of all the miracles and whatnot, so how could that work in a one-God culture. No one dared to re-raise the subject of multi-gods because Constantine had made it clear he'd had a gut full of the old ways and wanted progress.

Constantine himself was curious what the answer might be so he got three hundred bishops together for a month to decide it. Yes, you read right – three hundred. Christianity was big business now. But after a month of debate and gourmet food and wine, they still couldn't agree, so Constantine cancelled their expense accounts and gave them all a good bollocking for messing about on State funding. He ordered them to figure it out by the time he got back from the Senate, or there'd be trouble.

A week later there was still no agreement.

Fed-up to his chain mail with all their bishopy bullshit, he stormed in and did what they wouldn't. He decreed that there was only one God, and there would only ever be one God.

'But how do we explain Jesus?' asked one Bishop.

'God is God,' said Constantine. 'He can take whatever form He likes. He can appear as God the father of everything; He can appear as the man-shaped Jesus when it pleases Him; or He can exist as an all pervading mysterious invisible spirit without shape and substance whenever the situation calls for it. But get this, and get it good! God is not three different gods; He's just one God – the only one. He makes the rules in Heaven; I make them here on Earth. Understand?'

'But sire...' protested two bishops together, their words frozen to their lips as their instantly severed heads thumped wetly onto conference room note pads; officially marking the end of question time.

'Understand,' repeated Constantine, this time without a rising inflexion.

'Yes, all perfectly clear,' agreed the remaining two hundred and ninety eight Bishops. 'The father, the son and the holy ghost; a sort of holy trinity. We love it. Good job, sire.'

Madam Self Delusion pitched in to help the bishops grasp the concept of a Holy Trinity – that dad, junior and the spook were really all just one entity – even though it made no rational sense at all; but that's what she does best. It was all fine by me.

Meanwhile Constantine and I worked as a team to back her up. I reminded the bishops that they were going to die one day while Constantine unambiguously emphasised that if they didn't want it to be that day they'd better shut up and obey. His clear presentation of alternatives was so effective I adopted it as the preferred Christian dogma for the next thousand years until Martin Luther came along and threw a spanner into the works; but I wasn't to know he was coming, was I?

When I look back on my life even today, I consider my Holy Trinity version to be my finest work of trickery so far. The beauty of Trinity-me was that there was a little something in it for everyone. Mono-god lovers and stereo-god lovers alike could all dance to its tune; a song for all believers. The proof is in its survival. Trinity-me works as well today as it ever did because it's such a flexible arrangement. When people get jaded with an aloof invisible God who works in mysterious ways (read not in the ways they want) they can legally revert to idolatry by praying to a physical Jesus – a blond blue eyed type or a swarthy Mediterranean type or a stern Gothic type as their culture demands. Or they can use Charlton Heston's photo if the imagination struggles. As for the kiddies who ask their parents, 'how can God be everywhere?' they don't have to struggle with complicated stuff about chemical patterns and Morse Code and all that. All they have to be told is that I can turn into a spirit when I feel like it. And given the poor quality control over language then and now, spirits and ghosts have come to mean the same thing, so the kids now just imagine me as Casper. And that's the way things have stayed to this day.

Having done such great work, I reckoned I was due for promotion, and if my sept-centenarian cycle was correct, I had just four hundred years left to wait for the next version of me.

And what a ripper he turned out to be.

11

ME AND MO AND VENUS TOO

A lesson for all you soothsayers out there: when you predict something, never give an exact value. Give it a range instead. I knew the seven hundred year cycle had a plus or minus error-band over it, but seven is such a lucky number that I figured my next mutation would peak sometime in 700 AD. As it happened, he peaked a hundred years early.

I suppose I could make the excuse that with two hundred million heads to tend I was a tad busy, but these days I can quite happily juggle seven billion, so that can't be the reason. No, it wasn't a question of numbers; it was my own hubris, believing that I could predict things to the day, expecting that people would perform on cue. They never had so far, so why I expected this one to, I can't explain. Maybe it was because people are usually so late that subliminally I expected my next appointment would be late too. But then occasionally, just to mess with me, one arrives early. So when a guy with all the right doubts and questions came along a hundred years early, I very nearly missed him altogether. But thanks to Venus's coming to my rescue (the planet, not the de Milo) it all turned out very nicely in the end.

It happened in 610 when a chap with the longest business card in history was calling out to me for a sign. His name was Abu al-Qasim Muhammad Ibn Abd Allah Ibn Abd al-Muttalib Ibn Hashim. He was around forty years old when he called to me for help, which was surprisingly late for someone as well off as he was. Usually by that age people are pretty set in their ways and aren't looking for change. Granted he'd led a bit of an up and down life during the early part of his life, but eventually he'd landed on his feet and was doing quite well for himself. So his prayer didn't contain the usual *send me some money*, or *kill that bastard boss of mine*, and such like. No, his prayer was actually about me.

I mentioned his age because I think it was crucial in his decision to take over the world. You see by this time more and more people were living through their forties and discovering something hitherto unknown about growing old.

Since Muktuk's day the average lifespan of hominids had been increasing by about two years for every hundred thousand survived, so that by now, notwithstanding the dubious arithmetic of biblical characters, a really old person would be sixty. This opened up a whole swag of diseases for people to deal with that their younger, more accident-prone ancestors never lived long enough to experience. One such disease was the male midlife crisis, which attacks when men live too long beyond grand-parenting age.

Since male plumbing seems to have no expiry date, midlife means that men in their forties start to itch and squirm with the possibility of trying their luck with women a whole lot younger than the withered husk they're currently married to. They ache for a new beginning; to be born again so-to-speak and do something and someone new. These days the midlife crisis usually involves a Harley Davidson and a pole-dancer from Vegas; but in 610 the options were thankfully less embarrassing.

Something like a midlife crisis was happening to Abu al-Qasim Muhammad Ibn Abd Allah Ibn Abd al-Muttalib Ibn Hashim. Although born to a well-to-do family, he struck out early in life: once when mum and dad orphaned him by dying prematurely; and again when his older brother claimed the inheritance, and showed him the door. Consequently he had a pretty disillusioned view of life, wondering why Allah had forsaken him, and all the other things that disillusioned Arabs tended to wonder about while scavenging for scraps at the edge of town.

Then, during his thirties his luck changed. A rich woman took a shine to him, and changed his life. She liked the look of him and appreciated that he washed a lot and smelled nice, and was reasonably articulate and so on, so she gave him a job as courier *cum* security guard to escort her valuable produce to market. He turned out to be pretty good at it and other more personal things too, which prompted his new sugar-mummy to propose marriage, which he accepted, whereupon life became pretty cushy. But, as with Sharmah the Stone Age slacker who started all this, a cushy life meant plenty of time to sit around and think.

Abu al-Qasim Muhammad Ibn Abd Allah Ibn Abd al-Muttalib Ibn Hashim, hereinafter called Mo to save ink, was like every other married man on Earth – he needed a cave to escape to, from time to time, be it metaphorical or literal. In his case it was literal – he really did own his own cave in the desert where he would spend hours meditating and wondering what his selfish rich brother would think of him now.

One of the upsides of living in a desert (possibly the only one) is that you get to see all of the sky all of the time, day and night. The stars become very familiar friends, and when one of them does something unusual it gets your instant attention.

One morning, right on dawn, Mo was on his way home from his cave after a particularly heavy night of meditation when something in the sky caught his eye. It was the moon on the eastern horizon. Now Mo had seen the moon plenty of times before and didn't normally pay much attention to it, but this particular moon looked weird. It was one of those times when the sun and moon were going to rise about the same time but the sun was lagging by a few minutes so it was still below the horizon when the moon was just above it.

Even the least astronomically minded of you should know that when the sun rises it doesn't actually get switched on by a big light switch; it's been shining the whole time since it apparently dropped below the western horizon the night before. But with the Earth in your way you weren't able to see it during the night. The moon however, being a quarter million miles out in space doesn't have your problem. It sees the sun all the time, day and night, except for the occasional lunar eclipse when the Earth really does get in its way, but we can ignore those occasions for this discussion.

But even though the moon is nearly always bathed in sunshine and right there in front of your face when it's on your side of the Earth, sometimes you can't see it because all of the sun's light is shining on its back, and none of it is shining on the side facing you. When that happens, no matter how hard you look, you can't see it. But trust me it's still there. There's just nothing reflecting off it to give away its position. When people figured that out they called it a New Moon.

One such New Moon had occurred on the morning prior to Mo's observation. If he'd gone strolling on that morning he wouldn't have noticed anything unusual because there wouldn't have been anything to see. But he didn't; he went strolling the morning *after* New Moon, when the moon was one hand span above the horizon, and the light from the still-hidden sun was catching its underside. Pollution hadn't been invented yet so Mo had a clear view of the awesome sight: a beautiful golden sliver of moon slicing through the pre-dawn glow like a cupped hand rising majestically into the sky.

Since the invention of nail clippers, people have called that kind of moon a *fingernail moon*, but in Mo's day people needed their fingernails for all sorts of practical reasons that you'd rather not know about, so people didn't find neatly clipped nails on the bathroom floor like they do today. Hence the moon metaphor wasn't coined till much later. Instead people back then called this kind of moon a *boat moon*, because it looked for all the world like a boat floating along the horizon.

You don't get to see this phenomenon today because the neighbour's fence is in the way, and even if you go to the beach to look for it, pollution is always there to spoil the show. But back in Mo's day the air was crystal clear, and it was an awesome sight to see, impossible to ignore.

By the way, if you're wondering why the astronomy lesson, I'm getting to that. It wasn't the boat moon *per se* that stopped Mo in his tracks; he'd seen them before, too. What stopped him in his tracks was me playing tricks with his mind. You see the planet Venus happened to be in her brightest phase of the year, and by a stroke of pure Lotto luck she was lined up in such a way as to appear to be riding just above the boat moon.

Mo, of course, was no dill. He was at least as smart as most of his peers and quite a bit smarter than many of them, but I figured it was a good bet that he didn't know Venus was actually on the other side of the sun far, far away across the solar system some two hundred and fifty million kilometres distant. And since the moon was less than half a million clicks away, Venus's appearance on the boat was just a trick of three dimensional space painted on a two dimensional retina. Lucky for me, Mo didn't know any of that and like all smart people he started thinking of reasons to explain it.

This was the moment I'd been waiting for. It was a genuine Sharmah-and-the-snake moment. Mo wanted to understand what was happening so I told him. Before he got a chance to invent gravity and elliptical orbits and planetary occultations and all that, I gave him a much simpler explanation, knowing how people always prefer simplicity to accuracy.

I told him the apparition was my way of sending him a highly personalised message. I let him know I'd been listening to his prayer, but at the same time I couldn't just fly down from heaven and introduce myself because whenever I'd done that in the past it always freaked people out.

Mo was still in a post meditative daze so it wasn't difficult to gain his acceptance – a little pleasure here, a flash of awe there, a touch of you're the chosen one, etc and he was hooked.

I was well practiced at this by now, having pulled the same stunt on Saul while he'd been walking to Damascus; and Mo turned out to be equally receptive.

Coincidentally Mo, like Saul had similar issues with the prevailing religion of the day, and again like Saul, was ripe for plucking. Here's why.

In Mo's day, the parts of the Roman Empire that weren't already in tatters were now centred on old Greece, with Constantine's legacy, Constantinople its bustling capital. You won't know it as the Roman Empire, you'll know it as the Byzantine Empire, but despite the name-change it was as Roman as Romulus and Remus and SPQR.

Apart from Latin beginning to unravel into its many variants that would eventually become French, Italian, Spanish and English, nothing much else had changed since Constantine's day. Byzantium was still in a perpetual state of war with everyone, including but not limited to Germans (who wasn't?), Visigoths, Ostrogoths, West Goths, Franks, Vandals and Lombards; and further afield, Celts, Saxons, Burgundians and the last surviving Moors of original Mauritania. These were all tattered remnants of the original empire, so you could say the Romans had finally found a way to war with everyone including themselves. Everyone that is, except Arabia.

Arabia stayed out of the fight. While everyone was getting better and better at breaking things, the Arabs were getting better and better at making things: like coffee and chess and the pinhole camera and soap and windmills and alcohol distilleries and IOUs and better gunpowder and anaesthetized surgery and a huge list of inventions that others in the western world would later claim as their own. Arabia saved while others spent, so then, as now, while everyone else went bankrupt, Arabia got rich. The more astute of you will notice China doing the same thing today.

Arabian wealth led to Arabian prosperity, and the Arabs could have owned the world right then and there if they'd played their cards right. But the one thing they didn't invent (still haven't) was a governmental system capable of distributing wealth equitably, so politically things eventually went sour. Yes, prosperity bred wealth, but it also bred haves and have-nots; and true to form, the have-nots bred rebellion. Initially it was just whinging and whining rebellion, but soon it became real, honest-to-me, bloody rebellion.

And Mo was in the thick of it.

Further north among the warring tribes of Europe, Jesus-me had been spreading like measles and I was doing really well there, but in Arabia things were not so good. Arabs still considered themselves to be a descendent tribe of Abraham, one of the seven tribes that never found the imagined Promised Land for lack of long range helicopters. So in Arabia I still wore my old Jewish clothes, except for two minor modifications, which can be forgiven for lack of quality control.

Firstly, instead of whispering Yahweh under their breath the way Abe had demanded, these folks happily called me Allah out loud, and had already done so for a couple of centuries before Mo came on the scene. Secondly an early experiment of mine, in which I led them to believe I had daughter instead of a son, somehow got tangled up with the Holy Trinity story, the result being that while Christians insisted God-me had a son called Jesus, the Arabic Jews insisted that Allah-me had three daughters called Uzzah, Lat and Manat. Families, eh? You've gotta love 'em. This little bit of confusion led to some pretty interesting arguments around the oasis, but apart from those two minor oddities, I was still Jewish; as kosher as locks and bagels. Fortunately, Mo never really thought so.

By the way I was fine with Allah as another name. It meant one-god anyway, so it was perfectly in line with policy. Indeed its long trailing syllable was superior for spreading me about on horseback than was the more clipped god word that caught in the throat (another reason I never liked the word). Yahweeee would have done just fine because of its high pitched rising inflexion that carried nicely on the wind, but Abe's boycott on its use really killed any chance it might have had. Allaaaah was just as good, and in some ways even better because it rolled off the tongue nicely and carried from the throat forever. Moreover it was a close match to the tortured cries of those who would soon, albeit temporarily, refuse to say it.

At one time I tried joining all my names together into Joey God-Allah to form a sort of unified Jewchrislam Trinity to see if it would spread me around three times faster. But nobody took it seriously so I decided to let evolution decide which name would prevail. The battle continues.

So, back to Mo: all through his life he wanted to change things for the better, or rather to his particular version of better. Like many disillusioned Jews he had developed a bit of a soft spot for fundamentalist Christianity. Not the corrupt, bloated version I was using to spread myself around Europe, but the humble, by-the-book, do-unto-others version that Saul and I had concocted in Damascus three hundred years earlier, and which was still surviving well in North Africa. Mo even had a touch of the Jesus- complex about him, and frequently imagined himself presiding over flocks of faithful followers.

Understandably he was somewhat torn between religion and lifestyle. Given his intimate experience with poverty in early life, he didn't relish the idea of rocking the boat in his forties putting his guaranteed food supply at risk by denouncing the religion of his wife. His comfy life style relied on the *status quo* remaining as *status quo-y* as possible. Switching religions mid stream would surely set the camels amongst the date palms and foul the oasis forever.

This is precisely what he'd been meditating about all night in the cave, and it hadn't gotten him anywhere. By the wee small hours he'd given up meditating and resorted to out and out prayer, asking Allah-me for a sign. That was the instant I realized my seven hundred year clock was about to be reset.

Since Mo had been praying for a sign, the second he stepped out of his cave, I gave him one. And what a doozie it was. No, I'm not claiming credit for the moon-Venus alignment thing; the Great Random organizes stuff like that. It was just pure jaggy happenstance that GR's predawn sky-show was on. But I am definitely claiming credit for taking advantage.

I have to say I really love giving people a sign when they ask for one, because once they receive it they'll believe everything I tell them ever after. As soon as Mo beheld Venus bobbing along in her boat, I opened up a broadband channel directly into his self-esteem and started downloading everything I'd accumulated over the centuries.

Unfortunately his modem overloaded and he had a seizure not unlike the one Saul had endured six hundred years earlier. But Mo was a Jew with a strongly un-kosher interest in Christianity, so instead of having a simple stroke that clouded his vision like Saul had experienced back in the day, Mo created elaborate images inside his head instead – images he'd seen in books and parchments as a child. The most notable hallucination he enjoyed was that of the angel, Gabriel.

I can't claim full credit for this either, but I will surely share in some of it. Gabriel and all the other angels and demons and saints and whatnots decorating the frontispieces of bibles and prayer books since Saul's day were the direct outcome of hundreds of years of overactive human re-interpretation of Saul's (and my) letters.

Since Mo thought I was Gabriel speaking directly to him, I gave him a shot of oxytocin to convince him it was true, and we instantly morphed into a new version. Forever after he whole heartedly believed the angel Gabriel had given him permission – nay, instructions – to start a new religion.

Mo turned out to be prime real estate. He was so receptive to everything I downloaded, that he memorized it, wrote it down in a book and decided that everyone on earth had to memorize it too – or else.

I started by telling him he was my personal messenger and whatever he believed was right and good, and that everyone should be forced to believe it too. It was the usual stuff I tell people when they let down their guard, because it's precisely what they want to hear, and naturally he felt pretty good about it.

So far so good.

Then I poked around in his bias box and hit pay dirt. It turned out that he had a pre-existing, strongly held belief about the purpose of women, one that Raak would have understood completely, namely that a woman's place was below a man, both figuratively and literally, and if for some reason she forgot this natural law then the man was well within his rights to remind her in any way he deemed fit.

Some female readers will surely be offended by Mo's opinion of the purpose of women, and personally I don't blame them, but if I were forced to defend Mo's narrow misogynistic views I would offer the following.

Having studied the male mind since Muktuk had randy sons, I can say with very great certainty that men's views of women are largely in women's hands. Or to put it less succinctly: the more sex boys have with consenting girls, the more they'll like them; and, more importantly for world peace, the more docile they'll be – which has to be a good thing.

Unfortunately the reverse is also true. The less nooky they get, i.e. the more rejections they endure per successful mating, the more misogynistic they'll end up in later life, with a serious grudge against most other life forms too. This is not an immutable law of nature by any means, and I can sense you're already thinking up examples to refute me (I agree it's not universal – but then again what is?). But by and large the statistics will favour what I'm telling you.

So why am I telling you? Well, because it explains a lot about Mo himself and why he went on to choose a nine-year-old virgin (not necessarily tautological for the times) as a second wife. The little lass's name was Aisha, and she became instantly obedient, as she would. When you put a preteen up against a sex deprived quinquagenarian, rejection isn't likely to be the issue it used to be. The older party has the distinct advantage over the younger, and is free to work through his misogynous issues unchallenged. As I alluded to, this wasn't particularly new for the times. Mo certainly didn't invent such bad male behaviour, but he didn't try to stop it either, so baby brides were sanctioned in that part of the world for evermore. Nor did he stop at two wives. By the time I lost count he had somewhere between seven and eleven more as each got pregnant, died or just plain boring. Smart guy that he was in many things, he was a seriously slow learner in others, notably in avoiding domestic conflict. A harem is not the path to a quiet life.

But more importantly for the wider world, Mo's sexual issues in the Seventh Century explain quite a bit about events in the Twenty First; such as why some of his sex-deprived disciples would crash three aeroplanes into foreign buildings for no overtly obvious reason. But I was inside their heads while they were doing it, and I can tell you it was all about virgins. Virgins were all that their pinhole camera minds could focus on. The promise of being allowed to deflower them in Heaven was all that kept their otherwise immature self-esteems intact. This might surprise you because I know you've been told such terrorist activities are clumsy political statements. But to me the connection with virgins was clear as crystal. I'll explain why a moment and hopefully it will help female readers understand why I've been saying all along that they ought to put out a bit more generously than they currently do, that is if they want such violence to cease, which I'm not entirely convinced they do.

So who would have thought that answering a disillusioned Jew's prayer in the Seventh Century would have had such serious repercussions fourteen centuries later? What a waterbed life is? The sloshing never stops. And yes, this and much more still to come were a direct result of Mo's being a lousy date. Sharmah would have understood completely.

You see Mo's version of the afterlife was all about virgins. Well it would be wouldn't it. How else do you motivate young impressionable men to do your bidding? He promised seventy two virgins each to be exact, all standing at the gate with legs akimbo waiting for each new male arrival.

Below, you'll read what Mo wrote about his afterlife (Paradise, he called it), and while it's quite a bit more colourful than anything Sharmah could have dreamt up, I am still a little disappointed in it because it lacks a certain logic given that virginity is such a fleeting thing, while the stay in Paradise is quite a bit longer – eternity to be exact. Moreover he gives no hint of the source of all these virgins, nor what happens to them after they've been deflowered, although the glut of servants he mentions may point to the retirement plan for deflowered virgins. Worse still, his description doesn't offer much of a reward for women who aspire to go there (non lesbian ones at least) but in his defence it never occurred to him that women should be rewarded for anything anyway. Then again, maybe the virgins were boys. He never specified.

So, for better or worse, this is how Mo imagined his afterlife would be. It was his story, and I always try to keep out of the detail. Here is what he said:

The smallest reward for the people of Paradise is an abode where there are eighty thousand servants and seventy two virgins, over which stands a dome dripping with pearls, aquamarine and ruby, as wide as the distance from Damascus to Yemen.

Notwithstanding the blatant plagiarism of Valhalla adjusted for local gemstones, Mo's grasp of geography was a lot less grandiose than the Vikings'. His afterlife wasn't continent-sized but merely the size of the Arabian peninsular. Then again, he was describing the *smallest reward*, so who knows what he imagined the largest reward to be. And how did you get into this wonderful place? Well, by doing exactly what Mo (me actually) told you to do.

For the record, Mo's misogyny was always going to be inevitable. His mum dumped him in an orphanage when he was just a nipper and then died soon after without leaving him so much as a clean pair of socks. His grandfather took pity on the scrawny lad and gave him a rug to sleep on in the family tent till he was nine. But then granddad died too and his uncle took over the parental duty with considerably less enthusiasm. Uncle made sure little Mo didn't starve to death but that's about where his interest ended, and auntie wasn't too keen on raising someone else's kid either. Needless to say young Mo didn't grow up with a high opinion of human nature.

This alone would have been enough to warrant long-term therapy, but subsequent events absolutely clinched it. Being a sickly orphan for want of adequate nourishment and motherly love, and with no visible means of supporting himself let alone a wife, he was never going to be much of a catch for girls his age. He therefore developed a healthy contempt for them as he went through puberty and into manhood.

Never the most popular stud at the party, his self-esteem took a major kick in the nuts when he realized that unless he accepted marriage from the only woman who'd ever paid him much attention (the older woman of means I mentioned earlier, who fancied him as a toy-boy), then he was surely destined to live the awkward life of a bachelor and the target of scurrilous gossip in an age when even suspected homosexuality was a castratable offence. No wonder images of virgins preoccupied him.

So poor twenty-five-year-old Mo found it prudent to marry rich forty-year-old Sawda bint Zama. His cushy lifestyle thereafter became wholly dependent on the old bint. And nothing breeds resentment like dependence.

Mo's misogyny was just one of his many pathologies but it was the one that worked best for me. Given the propensity of most men to make fools of themselves over anyone sporting a vagina, it was easy enough to insert Mo's prejudices into the deal. I convinced him that anyone who disagreed with his well-adjusted opinion of women was a misguided, pussy-whipped wimp, and should be brought into line by force if necessary.

Henceforth his mission in life was to use any means necessary to make every man in the world believe what he believed. That way he could repair his battered self-esteem, and would never again be embarrassed about his poor record of pulling birds. And it didn't matter what women thought; their male superiors were fully authorised to remind them they were going to die one day – almost certainly by a man's hand if they didn't obey.

Brilliant, eh? In one fell swoop I'd halved the amount of effort required to spread me about, by getting impressionable blokes to do the work for me. Why hadn't I thought of this before? It was a very promising start for a new religion, and in Mo's zeal I sensed he was going to spread me around better than any previous host I'd ever had. To ensure he was wholly committed, I gave him pleasure shot after pleasure shot until he came in his pants. That's what I call religious ecstasy.

Since Mo already had a touch of fervour about him, I had a really good feeling about this new strain. He grabbed it with such enthusiasm that I just sat back and let him get to it. It was Mo himself who suggested calling it Islam, which meant *submit* in Arabic, giving it the perfect, built-in feedback mechanism. The name defined the expectation, needing no priest or rabbi to remind carriers what was expected of them. The religion was called Submit; what else could its practitioners do? In fact it was such a great concept that I seriously toyed with the idea of renaming Christianity as Kneel, until I realized that in the then-flourishing English language in Europe, it was phonetically indistinguishable from Neil (as in Armstrong) and would have surely annoyed everyone who'd already been called Christian in its honour.

As for using any and all means at his disposal, bible reading wasn't among them, so he made the same mistakes that Abe had made in his first attempted land grab at Arabia – almost to the letter. For about a year he tried to talk people into submitting to his views about him being the head of the mosque, and that everyone should listen to him and do what he said, and all that, but all he could attract were younger brothers and second sons of wealthy merchants doomed to miss out on the family inheritance like he had. He also attracted people who had been demoted out of the first rank in their tribe or had failed to attain rank at all; as well as weak and unprotected foreigners. In other words, losers with a grudge.

Current Muslims don't have to be offended by this since losers were Abe's and Saul's preferred audience too. The downtrodden are just folks looking for ways to become high steppin', and if they play their cards right many of them will make that transition before they die, and declare their lives to be successful as they cease to be. It's a consistent promise I've made down the ages: *blessed are the meek for they shall inherit the Earth,* of words to that effect. All I have to do is offer the meek riches beyond wildest dreams, and I've got 'em.

The trouble with Mo was that he didn't have the means to deliver riches to anyone because they belonged to the Mrs, so his credibility dwindled dangerously. He couldn't really offer his followers much more than what they already had, which is to say: nothing. This depressed him a lot, so he started a kind of Robin Hood movement – stealing from the rich (i.e. Jewish merchants) and giving to the poor (i.e. his followers) who soon got the gist and followed his lead by stealing from the rich and keeping it for themselves.

Meccans (folks who lived in Mecca) got more than a little annoyed at Mo's unsociable approach to wealth redistribution, and were downright livid about his pretending that his Allah was better than their Allah and had stricter rules for Paradise, and better looking virgins and so on. I didn't mind of course, since both Allahs were me anyway, but the Meccans chose to be furious about it and started attacking Mo from all sides. Since Mo hadn't properly equipped himself for war he decided to do an Abe, and run.

He led his sorry band of followers from the desert town of Mecca where no one liked them, to the desert town of Medina where no one liked them either. Medina was the agricultural centre of Arabia – a small but fertile oasis of limited resources – where Mo's mob was made about as welcome as a horde of gypsies camping on your front lawn.

But by a stroke of luck, the Medinans were already involved in a series of land-grab skirmishes of their own, so Mo volunteered his services as a wise and unbiased adjudicator willing to help sort the mess out. He was fifty-five by then and since age carried the same illusion of wisdom as it does now, the Medinans took him up on the offer. We were in!

The first thing we did was a Saul. We wrote down a whole bunch of rules and laws whereby Medinans might live together in harmony rather than raping and pillaging each other – a concept that had never occurred to them before. And they quite liked it for a while. We also slipped in a few clauses about letting Mo's people live on the outskirts of town without being spat on all the time. And that worked for a while too.

The trouble with having laws is that when you want to create havoc, it's so easy to break one and then blame someone else for it. If you're really good at it (ref. CIA Standard Operating Manual, Vol. 1, Clause 1) you can get peace-loving people tearing at each other's throats in no time at all; and during the mayhem you can take what you want without anyone noticing. This is precisely what transpired a couple years after Mo set up shop in Medina, and Mo got blamed for all of it.

Despite the veneer of tolerance he was trying to engender, too many people contesting too few resources was always going to result in haves and have nots. Mo could see it coming and got depressed about it, and even partook of a few half-hearted skirmishes of his own to keep his followers fed. But nothing much came of them and for a while it looked like Mo was destined for the scrap heap of *nearly made it*.

After putting up with a couple of years of Mo's self pity and his incessant moaning about how ungrateful people were and how they wouldn't do what he told them to do, I finally got it through his thick scull that we needed a more structured approach. I suggested a tactic that was working brilliantly for me in Europe, notably violence, but not just any old violence; I was talking violence on a grand scale.

By then Mo was well into his grumpy fifties and was sick and tired of young hotshots getting better deals and prettier girls than he was getting, so he embraced my suggestion with an enthusiasm that would have thrilled Abraham.

Since there were far more have-nots than haves, Mo went about raising an army of the former, hell bent on becoming the latter, and took over Media in about ten seconds flat, putting himself in charge of everything, Sargon-style.

Now we were off to the races – finally! We led the power-drunk army back to Mecca for a bit of revenge where we slaughtered everyone who said they didn't like us, until the remaining survivors said they did. Then to keep the momentum going we spread all over the Arabian peninsular screaming *submit* at the top of our voices and decapitating anyone who wouldn't. We were screaming in Arabic of course, so Islam caught on in a big way. It had to. Unnatural selection made sure of it. Headstrong non-submissives became headless non-submissives at the swipe of a scimitar, and thus went extinct overnight; while headweak submissives survived to beget more of themselves and thus became the submissive Islam of today. Then, as now, success was measured by headcount.

I was in my own private (dare I say it?) *heaven*. This was a far more effective way of spreading myself around than lecturing, discussing, cajoling, threatening or even torturing, which were time-consuming at best and extremely messy at worst. How much easier to simply eradicate the competition then wait nine months for the survivors' progeny to fill the gaps.

When I look back to this period in history, I still consider the sieges and slaughters of Mecca, Medina and Badr – in which a quarter of all Arabs were slaughtered in my name – to be the finest examples of social Darwinism ever perpetrated, although I would have to wait fourteen hundred years for Charles to write his infernal book and thus enable me to describe it so. Incidentally Charles Darwin's views are also partly thanks to me, but more on him later. For the time being let it be said that Mo was the first true Darwinist; a man seriously ahead of his time.

That Mo heeded my suggestion of violence was entirely predictable. Humans (in case you're not one reading this) have violence encoded into their operating system. Ask anyone who's discovered that some inconsiderate asshole has parked his car across their driveway. They'll back me up on this. Aware of their blood-soaked history, humans desperately try to avoid violence and call the police instead. It's not because they are cowards; it's because somewhere deep down they know that if they pop their corks, things will go from bad to worse very quickly. Many people think the 'worse' is that once they start they won't be able to stop; that their rage will spurt like champagne and never be put back. But they're wrong.

The real problem is they won't be able to keep it up. Violence is virtually impossible for humans to maintain 24/7. They know that sooner or later they'll get sick of it and want to settle down on the farm and grow food and raise kids and all that, which they really can't do while spending day and night fending off others being violent in return. Violence sounds good (and by all accounts feels good too) but sooner or later it peters out leaving a worse mess to clean up than the one you started with.

Plenty of violence-based endeavours have proved this to be the case time and time again, such as the Viking invasions of Britain; the British invasions of India, Australia and North America; the Spanish Invasion of South America, the Dutch invasion of Indonesia; Genghis Khan's Excellent Asian Adventure – I could go on. These were pretty violent endeavours in anyone's book, but none of the perpetrators could keep the violence going for very long, historically speaking. After a while people just got fed up with the violence, and called barleese [look it up]. They collectively agreed to resort to an imperfect non-violence based society, and to live with the inevitable frustration that comes with it. So when the driveway is blocked they don't reach for a gun, they reach for a telephone; grin and bear it; and call the police instead.

Nevertheless the lust for violence lurks just below the tissue-thin veneer of grin-and-bear-it tolerance demanded by society. All it takes is for someone in authority to give violence the all-clear then it's on for young and old for as long as people can sustain it. During such excursions there'll be no end to the evil schemes people will dream up to feed their blood lust. This is exactly what I did for Mo, and he took the bait right down to the swivel.

I gave him a double-oh rating – a license to kill whomever the heck he felt like if they wouldn't obey us. We agreed that my proliferation was much more important than the wretched lives of a few recalcitrant Jews who wouldn't submit, so anyone who offended us could be regarded as fair game, provided it helped to spread me about.

I gave him *carte-blanche* to dispatch anyone for the cause, and although murder was, deep down, against his better judgment (a throw-back to Moses and our ten commandments) Madam Self Delusion was right there backing me up, assuring him it was all for the greater good. She convinced Mo that I had reserved the top spot for him in paradise irrespective of any murderous activities he perpetrated here on Earth. She stroked his self-esteem with reassurances that the important work he was doing in this world amounted to a free pass into the next, no matter what he did. And like every other human I've ever inhabited, permission to murder with impunity was just too much of a temptation. The poor darling bought it hook, line and Koran. What a sucker.

During the entire period of this deception Mo did great work for me, and his contribution to my dominion over humanity has been truly invaluable. Once unleashed, Mo's militia rampaged across the Arabian peninsular killing everyone who wouldn't submit, and quite a few slow deciders just to keep in practice, making us more feared than smallpox and a lot more virulent. Within two years, the new Muslim version of Allah-me was the only god that survivors were allowed to worship, making the whole country instantly submissive – or Islamic, if you will. It was the second fastest wholesale change of religion in history, beaten only by Constantine's government-led conversions. Sharmah would have had an orgasm.

But given that Mo had inherited the Sharmah syndrome to an even greater degree, his sense of self-importance swelled like dropsy. No quiet prayers for Mo. From now on people would have to show their devotion overtly and vociferously by praying in the direction of Mo's home town of Mecca instead of the out-dated crumbling town of Jerusalem. Moreover they would have to pray at least five times a day – at predawn, at noon, sometime in the afternoon, at sunset and at night. Otherwise the neighbours were well within their rights to dob them in for a stoning. Islam was here to stay.

But in making everyone submissive we had seriously reduced the population, and propagation of any virus needs a large population. This is where you come in.

One of the nice things about humans is that they keep making more humans. It only takes nine months to make a new one so there's always a regular crop sprouting for me to tend. But the downside is it's always an imperfect crop. They're all empty-headed mutants, every one of them.

You'd think after all this time evolution would have found a way for someone's snotty little sprog to mutate so it remembered everything its parents already knew, wouldn't you? It can't be that hard for DNA to master such a seemingly simple task. It manages to replicate the brain itself, which is far more complex and subject to far more potential errors; yet most brains usually come out all right, so why not their contents too?

But oh no; it's always a funny little nose, or an eleventh finger or some such waste of a good mutation, never a pre-loaded brain. What a half-baked arrangement heredity is. Every baby I've seen has popped out with a completely empty brain, save for a few BIOS settings like *suck* and *cry* which don't help my cause one megabyte, so I'm constantly faced with the problem of how to program the little blighters before they get ideas of their own.

Since Muktuk's time, mums and dads have been reasonably good programmers because kids, during their brain-wiring years, will download pretty well everything their parents tell them. This is when I set healthy roots; but the little ankle biters never seem to get it word perfect; and worse still, as they get older, a rebellious phase kicks in resulting in ten to fifteen percent of teenagers being defective carriers.

I am powerless to prevent this because I can't re-wire brains from the inside. It has to be done through the eyes and ears, to which I have limited access. I don't mind a small number going feral because that is after all where my next strain will come from, but ten to fifteen percent is too much. I want nearly zero defects – one or twp percent at most. Neither Sharmah, nor Abe, nor Moses, nor Saul ever found a way to keep all teenagers on the straight and narrow. But here at last in Islam, I saw my best chance. Here's why.

I mentioned already that I'd given Mo a double-oh license that made it OK to kill people who didn't behave, while reassuring him his seventy two virgins awaited him in heaven. But unfortunately the licence came with a loophole. It turned out that parents were a tad squeamish about butchering their own issue irrespective of how recalcitrant the little ingrates were. Fatal violence just didn't seem to work inside the family unit, so I had to come up with another way.

Lo and behold it was easier than I expected – again thanks to you. The answer was of course, sex. You see Muslim daughters aren't nearly as defiant as Muslim sons. Defiant sons outnumber defiant daughters by a ratio of over four to one, so a lot more defiant boys grow into defiant men with a touch of the rebel in them. But they also grow up with a touch of the randy in them, and you can take it from someone who's been around for a million years, randy always wins.

Youths aren't Einsteins at the best of times, but when one of them sees a drop-dead gorgeous, scantily veiled honey-pot who whispers into his ear that her seventh veil had gone all moist for him, he loses half his IQ points, drools inanely and comes in his pants.

Then follows a time-honoured ironclad process that survives to the present day: daughter tells mum; mum tells dad; dad confronts youth; youth asks for daughter's hand and everything connected to it; dad sets one condition that turns out to be thousands, which is that youth must embrace all family traditions including Islam; youth hesitates for a moment; dad points to scimitar over fireplace capable of beheading elephants; youth is converted.

With a process like this in place, Mo only had to transmit me into husbands, and the rest of the family followed like baggage carts. All husbands had to do was insert me forcibly into their wives (often literally); wives would then instil me into their daughters with a stern warning about what dad might do if she didn't obey; then daughters would use their juicy powers of persuasion to transmit me sexually into their randy boyfriends. Who'd have thought, eh? After a million years I'd finally become a sexually transmitted disease. *Submit* is such a great word.

Hallelujah, Hallelujah, Hallelujah.

Well, with 100% of Arabs thus converted in record time, it was time to head north. If we could conquer Constantinople we'd be on our way to Europe and to a showdown with Jesus-me that I simply couldn't lose. It would be the mother of all Crusades with plenty of land-grabbing, pillaging and raping along the way to sweeten the pot. Again I say Hallelujah, Hallelujah, Hallelujah.

But as things turned out Mo's Arabian knights never did take Constantinople away from the Christians in his lifetime. The Byzantines were a stubborn and sturdy lot from hardy Greco-Roman stock, who successfully repelled attack after attack until eventually Mo died in 632 AD at the age of sixty-two still preaching to the converted, so he never did complete the mission I'd set for him.

Unwisely he died without having written a Will, so his death opened the door for a family squabble of absolutely Koranic proportions. You see, by now little Aisha was in her twenties. Mo had treated her like a child (well, he would wouldn't he) so she suffered the same shortcoming that any dominated wife suffers even today – she lost her power base when she became a widow. Nevertheless she had a few grownup ideas of her own.

To keep things in the family, Aisha declared that her father Abu Bakr was Mo's chosen successor as the next spiritual leader of Islam. But not everyone in the family agreed, especially as Abu Bakr – being merely Mo's father-in-law – wasn't a blood relative of the great man.

Mo's cousin Ali, who was also Mo's son-in-law since he'd married one of Mo's daughters, reckoned he was more in line for the big job, and insisted that he and his descendants, not Aisha and her descendents, should continue the family tradition. Families, eh? Such intrigue.

Aisha got pretty upset at Ali's defiance, not to mention a tad humiliated since, if you work through the genealogy, Ali was also her step-son-in-law, and no step-mother likes to be bullied by a step-child, irrespective of dubious bloodline.

It all came to a head in a bloody, three-day skirmish called the Battle of the Camel, just outside the city of Basra. In the mayhem, Muslim happily killed Muslim – a tradition that continues to this day when there aren't any Infidels around – but neither side could keep up the violence long enough to reach a definitive outcome. It was just another one of history's many lose-lose situations, so each side declared themselves the winner, and as a result the Sunnis (Aisha's lot) and the Shiites (Ali's lot) simply agreed to hate each other from then on – an agreement both sides have faithfully kept.

Nevertheless, despite the family squabble Mo caused by dying intestate, he inspired several non-relative groups to keep their eye on the main event, which was Constantinople.

One such inspired group was a small band of Seljuks from Turkmenistan to whom I promised the usual booty of heavenly life, luxury and willing virgins if they converted to Islam. They liked the idea so much they started attacking Constantinople straight away.

These Ottomans as they called themselves, turned out to be a good find. Despite their octagonal name they were no footstools. They embraced Allah-me with a vengeance that would have made Mo proud if he'd lived long enough to see it. But despite their violent enthusiasm they underestimated Byzantine stubbornness, and wars raged for centuries, seven of them if fact.

Inspired with a never-give-up attitude, the Ottomans actually really did take seven hundred years of skirmishes, sieges and full scale wars to wear down Byzantine resolve. But eventually they did it – they captured Constantinople after killing the last Roman emperor ever to walk the earth; and in doing so put a final and humiliating end to the once proud Roman Empire. That has to count for something.

The particular emperor they killed was called Constantine XI, and since Constantinople really just meant Constantine's City, in yet another example of unimaginative nomenclature, the Ottomans simply dropped the Constantine part and renamed it City, which in the Greek being spoken at the time translated as Istanbul. After all that trouble wouldn't you think they'd have come up with a better name than City? Where had imagination gone?

Well regardless of what they called it, they were true Mo's inspiration and made Istanbul as Islamic as blue tiles. And they've never let go of it since, not even after several horrendously brutal crusades by European Christians who wanted it back. Nevertheless, Istanbul is pretty much where we stopped. As Allah-me, I never exploded into Europe the way Mo and I had envisaged. Instead I began seeping in like ink up blotting paper – advance scouts, you might say, for explosions still to come.

I often speculate on how humanity might turned out if Mo had gone meditating a day earlier or a day later; if he'd stepped out of the cave to go home to his bint with nothing special in the sky to enthral him. Could I have found another sign to answer his prayer – a fortuitous meteor perhaps, or a flock of geese flying in the shape of a camel; maybe a blinding headache or a flash of light? I don't know – they might not have been quite enough. I suspect Mo needed a real blockbuster like Venus in the boat to make him defect from his Judeo-Christian mishmash. Anything less probably wouldn't have tipped him over the edge.

Without my sign Islam might never have happened and I might never have had that willing crop of minds to feast on. There would have been no artistic explosion of beautiful Islamic architecture by talented builders; no concrete explosions of Western architecture by terrorist bombers; no reason for the Normans to go crusading, no Richard the Lion Heart. And no 9/11 either.

Then again, I don't think it would have mattered that much if it had been someone else instead of Mo – people being the habitual malcontents that they are. Someone else would have felt hard enough done by to pray to me for a sign at the precise moment a spectacular one was available, in which case I'd have swooped in most eagerly.

And who knows: it might have been a disillusioned Mongol soldier fed up with sweeping the Asian steppes for Empress Wu Zetien? He might have opened up China for me – the Holy Grail of malleable minds on the planet.

Or perhaps the cycle might have skipped a turn. I might have had to wait another seven hundred years. Maybe I could have talked Thomas de Torquemada into creating a strain based on institutionalised mutilation and torture? Or I might have been alert to some disenchanted Buddhist reluctantly spinning his prayer wheels, convincing him to turn him to the Dark Side.

Any number of permutations is possible, and with the right one I might already be the absolute ruler of all minds human, instead of an idea evolving slowly but inexorably forward in seven hundred year increments toward that same end. Oh, well, if a million years teaches you anything, it's patience. We all have our dreams but reality is reality whichever way you spell it. Mo chose the day after New Moon, and that was that.

12

MARTY, MYSOGENY AND MAGIC MUSHROOMS

After nearly missing the previous cycle by a hundred years I made sure I was better prepared for the next one. Allowing for a full century of uncertainty in my calculations, the seven-hundred-year window should have opened around 1210, six hundred years after the Islamic ball started rolling. Of course I couldn't be sure exactly *where* the window of opportunity would open, but Africa seemed like a good bet since Islam had been roaring across it like fire in dry grass. My guess was Ethiopia because the Horn of Africa was one of Islam's early injection points into that Dark Continent, being a mere head-kick across the narrow *Bab el Mandeb* strait from Arabia. It seemed the obvious place for Islamic dissatisfaction to begin festering given it had been stewing there the longest.

Actually, guessing where it would happen was just for personal amusement; it was of no material importance. It would happen where it happened. *When* was of more interest to me because I didn't want to be unprepared. When the prescribed moment arrived I would start probing minds simultaneously across the entire human race looking for the inevitable chinks of dissatisfaction.

Starting on January 1st, 1210, I probed and I prodded and I looked and I lurked. And when I found no one ready to split I did it all over again.

Well, as luck would have it (bad luck that is) the wave slopped the other way this time and the window opened a couple hundred years late, proving yet again that people can't be trusted. Three hundred years after I started looking I finally got a hit, in 1571 AD to be precise, and in Germany of all places. Plus I got the strain wrong as well. The mutation affected Christian-me, not Muslim-me as I'd been expecting. Prediction obviously isn't my long suit.

In hindsight Christianity was ripe for revolution and I should have guessed that's where it would happen. God-me had been stewing a lot longer than Allah-me, and therefore had cooked up several new recipes. Saul's original Christianity was completely unrecognisable by now, with its dominant form calling itself Catholicism. There had been three main forms since Constantine: Gnostic, Orthodox and Catholic, each vying for dominance; and as in most things human, the most brutal dominated.

Successive Catholic popes systematically killed off Gnostic and Orthodox leaders who tried to arrange civilized leadership discussions; and banished surviving followers of those strains to tiny corners of Egypt and Greece where they laid low and kept out of trouble.

But it wasn't all roses on Vatican Hill either, with internal fighting and fierce backstabbing (literally) deciding papal longevity. For example during the seventh century while Mo and I were in our heyday down in Mecca, twenty Catholic popes in Europe came and went in the space of a hundred years; with ten of them clinging to the throne for less than two years each. Life was pretty tough at the top.

Initially Catholicism was merely a minor variation on a theme, and didn't justify my wholesale intervention. It appeared to be conforming to my strict policy of disseminating me into every mind it could lay its Catechisms on so its internal wranglings were irrelevant to the cause. Indeed for a while Catholics did pretty well, crawling all over Europe like ants on a corpse, and their self-appointed leaders held great power. But with great power comes great... yeah, yeah, you know already.

Responsibility followed its normal pattern: power; abuse; downfall.

By medieval times, gluttony and boozy orgies had become standard Friday night fare among Catholic leaders, with bishops, priests and deacons quite happily screwing everything on two legs during the week in preparation for renewing their vows of abstinence on Sunday.

Actually such behaviour had been going on ever since Constantine converted, but had been sensibly kept out of sight until the Ninth Century when the English-born pope, Pope John spectacularly failed a celibacy test (and a gender test as things turned out) by giving birth to a baby boy before he/she could reach the safe haven of his/her Vatican palace, whereupon he/she was nicknamed Pope Joan, and stoned to a pulp by his/her followers who didn't appreciate being duped.

Indeed the folks back then were so outraged by the shocking deception that ever since that day, would-be popes have had their family jewels closely scrutinized by a committee, once more demonstrating the clergy's ingrained fascination with male genitalia. Even Saul's noble idea of tuning the other cheek had become a smutty, below the belt fart joke and forerunner of centuries of tedious British toilet humour still to come. Mind you it had no effect on the sexual interests of the clergy. All it did was bring it out into the open. Who says religion can't be fun?

Personally I was OK with all this, but what got up my imaginary nose was that rich Catholics had come up with a way of avoiding being humble and submissive to me. They decided they could commit any sin they liked and then buy it back on a kind of hire-purchase plan. What was the point of having rules if you could buy your way around them? Humility and submission had become a thing of the past, and as I mentioned earlier, submission was key to my proliferation.

Rich blokes could now root the neighbour's wife on Friday, pop along to confession on Saturday, slip the priest a fiver through the grille then wait till Monday for the next neighbourly go-round. Sunday was really the only day of rest.

This pay-as-you-sin practice, which Pope Urban II called *indulgences* (a surprisingly honest and damning description I thought) was a clear demonstration of just how much he didn't care what people thought of him. Indulgences were nothing short of a tax on sin, collectible by the Church rather than by government since the Church *was* the government. Sharmah would have been so proud.

The business of Indulgences was massively lucrative. It was how popes funded themselves and capital projects such as cathedrals and presbyteries and St Peter's Basilica, not to mention numerous seminaries (another apt word when you think about what all those young priests got up to), and of course the dubious practices that went on inside them. Naturally, Indulgences weren't billed as a tax; they were billed as an investment in your future, redeemable only after you die. Today you'd call it extortion.

I'm sure you recognize *indulgences* as just an up-scaled version of Sharmah-the-stinky's grave offerings for entering the afterlife, but Pope Urban wasn't interested in spears or mammoth fur; he wanted cold hard cash, and when he couldn't get cash then a lifetime of plundering Muslims on his behalf i.e. Crusades, would suffice. He argued that indulgences were merely what popes deserved given they had a direct line to the Supreme Being.

If the popes of the time really did believe in a supreme being, they surely missed the signs that they'd made it angry. Whenever the Black Death plague visited down upon their heads, which it did regularly, it systematically attacked the clergy more than any other profession. You'd have thought some priest or bishop might have suspected they were all being targeted, and mentioned it before he died. But no, the clergy obstinately stuck to its practices, dare I say, religiously.

As far as I could tell, a supreme being wasn't actually targeting them, it just looked that way. I was the only supreme being they'd ever been told existed anyway, and it certainly wasn't my doing. My powers as you've already seen are limited to tweaking gullible minds into doing whatever I want them to do. I definitely have no effect on bacteria. I can't tell *Yersinia pestis* whom it can and can't infect, or when. Besides, why would I want it to attack carriers of my own particular mind virus?

No, the plague, like almost everything else, was not my fault; the Great Random looks after such things. As far as I could tell, the plague was purely a consequence of too many people living with too many rats, too close to each other in dubious states of cleanliness. But it wasn't really the rats' fault either. Rats were just as vulnerable to plague as people, and suffered the same dreadful fate, with more rats dying of it than people.

Even the poor old flea who got blamed for spreading plague about was harshly branded in my opinion. Fleas that lived on infected rat blood got infected too, and thereafter found dead rat blood quite distasteful. But when they switched to your blood as an alternative food source, they found they couldn't swallow it because *Yersinia pestis* had given them the mother of sore throats. What else could they do but vomit it back, with sneaky *Yersinia pestis* hitching a free ride into your bloodstream? The rats and the fleas died too you know, so why vilify them? Humans should really take more care when branding their enemies.

While on the subject of rats; having studied humankind for a long time now, I have to say that the poor old rat gets unjustly blamed for an awful lot of things that aren't really its fault, any more than say, being blown up by a letter bomb is the fault of the Post Office. Sometimes there are unwilling and unwitting carriers who can't be held accountable. For all the blame and derision heaped on *Ratus ratus* and his various cousins, the worst thing he can do unaided is eat you when there's nothing else available – which is pretty bad I suppose for the person being eaten – but it rarely happens, except on battlefields where it's often a blessing.

No, despite what you've been taught, rats aren't to blame for the plague; humans are. Yes, it was you. You see back in the fifteen hundreds, cleanliness wasn't even close to godliness.

People, it turns out, are toxic to each other and should really keep their distance unless they're deliberately trying to create or end life. Other than those specific times where close proximity is largely unavoidable, people ought to limit their exposure to the poison that is other people. But back in the Middle Ages they were doing the exact opposite, and none more so than the clergy who positively excelled at it by cramming dozens and sometimes hundreds of grubby little men into monasteries, seminaries, vestries, churches, chapels and so on; plus quite a few women into convents and nunneries that were not as gender restricted as they pretended to be.

To make matters worse, thanks to their seemingly unstoppable fixation with the foreskin, priests declared washing anywhere near one as ungodly and tempting of the devil's hand (yeah right) and thus turned the crotch into an ideal breeding ground for just about everything that crawled. You guys really are something.

So what does this have to do with the pope's Indulgences? After the plague petered out, there simply weren't enough priests left alive to collect Indulgences. To fill the gap, the Vatican hired professional pardoners to collect them on the pope's behalf, allowing pardoners to take a slice of the pie as commission. I'm not sure the pope realized it at the time, but in doing so he handed the pardoners a veritable bird's nest on the ground – a goose that laid golden eggs on demand.

It was a totally unregulated practice so free enterprise kicked-in straight away. Professional pardoners immediately realized they could boost profits and have a little fun along the way by declaring more and more things as being sinful – such as reading and writing and being a woman and asking questions and not answering questions and not answering questions the right way and not admitting you're a witch and not having sex with professional pardoners, and on and on and on.

They even (cleverly in my view) expanded the market to dead people whom they claimed were trapped in a place called Purgatory – a kind of unpleasantly hot departure lounge poised between heaven and hell – where sinners waited in prickly discomfort for their rich Earthly relatives to buy them a ticket to heaven. The pardoning industry even commissioned a catchy jingle to promote the product:

As soon as a coin in the coffer rings,
A tortured soul from Purgatory springs.

You see this was the 16th Century, the height of the Catholic Inquisitions, so reigning popes had absolute power to do whatever they wanted. It was a golden age of papal wealth and power, which lasted over three hundred years; and even when the Inquisition was nearing its end in the 1800's (yes that late) it still packed a punch. But in the 16th and 17th Centuries the Inquisition was in its supreme heyday.

For example, in 1632, Pope Urban VIII happily escorted a seventy-year-old man into a torture chamber to show him which particular iron chair would be used to break the old man's legs if he didn't agree with the pope's theory that the sun went around the earth, and not the other way around.

Galileo Galilei was that seventy-year-old man, and even at that age he was about a trillion times smarter than Urban. He was also an accomplished mechanical engineer, so he didn't need to be told how the chair worked. But in case he had any doubts, Urban gleefully described its action while I played a movie inside Galileo's head.

The movie showed Galileo sitting naked in the freezing dungeon with his wrists secured to the armrests and his legs shackled in front of the chair's massive iron legs. At Urban's nod a horizontal iron blade would be cranked against Galileo's seventy-year-old shins until he either agreed with Urban's view of the solar system, or the iron bar reached the legs of the chair.

Being a doctor of medicine too, Galileo understood where all this was going and wisely took my advice to agree with Urban, but the torture-happy pope was just getting warmed up, and gave Galileo highly graphic descriptions of many other delights that awaited him if he dared study astronomy ever again.

This, by the way, was not an isolated event in history and clearly demonstrates what I've been telling you all along: people hate being disagreed with because it really messes with their self-esteem. Once Galileo saw what Urban had in store for him, he quite sensibly gave up astronomy altogether.

The reasons for Galileo's forced retirement spread through Europe like wildfire. All science ceased overnight in Catholic countries, and wouldn't start up again in Italy until the mid 18th Century when Alessandro Volta and Luigi Galvanni would simultaneously discover electricity, but by then the epicentre of science had shifted to northern Europe, never to return. Papal self-esteem thus remained intact for all that time.

To avoid an X-rating I shan't describe any more of the torture instruments designed and used by popes and their inquisitors, nor shall I go into any details of the horrors inflicted. If that sort of thing appeals the less squeamish of you can always Google them. Suffice to say that Catholic Inquisitions make the Nazi Holocaust look like kindergarten playtime. And if you think I'm exaggerating, here is a quotation that might get through the censors. It is a translation of a written report provided by the Grand Papal Auditor who went to France in 1480 to check on progress in expunging heretics (i.e. women).

'As we approached the observing room I heard a sound I could not recognize precisely, which I likened to a pig having skin peeled from its flesh while it still lived. I have extracted confessions from heretics many times myself, but these inhuman screams gave my hardened nerves cause to contract. Only the bliss of knowing that one more witch was being banished to Hell comforted me. Upon opening the heavy wooden doors, the screaming

grew a hundredfold, and I beheld the source of that hideous sound. It appeared to be a large red octopus that was being readied for cooking on an oddly low bench; and whose tentacles hung over the edges but did not reach the floor. Since its howls afforded no quiet space to allow me to question my guide as to why I had been brought to a kitchen, I walked closer to inspect the beast. The thick smell of burnt meat assailed my nostrils but did not seem to trouble three deacons standing about the bench. One stood aside to afford me closer inspection but chose not to remove his quivering hand from beneath his robe. Only then did I see what I had mistaken for a squirming octopus was in fact a bald woman whose four limbs had been wrenched free of their joints to slump uselessly down onto charcoal braziers spitting foul fat from her charred appendages. Her attempts to lift her useless limbs from the unavoidable coals caused muscles to jerk and convulse incessantly and violently, magnifying the agony of dislocation manifold. The screaming wretch was naked but I was relieved to see that her perverting breasts had been pared away to expose her dung-filled innards, thus accounting for the profusion of red covering her drenched torso. I was surprised at first to observe that her demonic nether region had been spared inquiry, but on closer inspection the blackness I mistook for hair was in fact searing charcoal nearly spent. That she still lived after such inquiry was proof enough of her guilt, but her witchcraft was plainly written for all to see in the once whites of her eyes now glowing red as the devil she worshiped. I offered her the grace of Your Holiness if she confessed her heresy, but she returned no words of repentance for her heretical profanations, so I left her to endure her plight. Outside where the air was quieter, I asked my guide what progress had been made since the Inquisitor heard her case. He replied that the Inquisitor was too busy with matters of state to try witches in person; instead he had read the charges elsewhere and found her guilty in absentia. Again I asked what progress, and my guide replied that the witch had revealed the names and hides of her coven, including her eight *children, three sisters and their perverted offspring, all of whom now await sentence. The husband, a man of good standing in Indulgences, has been granted entry to heaven if he informs us of ninety-nine more witches, and makes the offering. Your Holiness, this is clearly an unacceptable state of affairs. Inquisitors are spent to exhaustion, and I seek your leave to allow lesser priests and deacons to ease their considerable burden.'*

It wasn't the morality of these practices that annoyed me. I don't really care how people occupy themselves between birth and death. What got my attention was that I was no longer being spread around efficiently. You might be surprised to hear me say that, given the Church had reached the point of outsourcing operational procedures to sub- contractors, but the reality was that people were actually getting a little smarter. The tiniest bit of public education was beginning to appear around this time, and people were beginning to grasp the awful truth that their supposedly wonderful church leaders were probably insane.

I know how hard it is for humans to admit they are wrong; that they have been duped by people they once trusted; that they are too embarrassed to admit they let crazy people trick them into doing things that didn't feel right at the time. We've been through this before on the river of trust I mentioned earlier, and the only reason I mention it again is that elevated self-esteem can turn people into slow learners, and often the simplest concepts need hammering home.

Madam Self Delusion will assure such troubled egos that their original bad decision was a good one, despite mounting evidence to the contrary that they've been completely suckered. Most people re-succumb to her charms almost immediately, but just occasionally someone will swallow their pride and admit out loud that they've made a bad mistake, and demand that things must change. Under those circumstances, and if they can get the safety of numbers on their side, thousands if not millions will rebel with them.

The problem was that back in medieval times there was a shortage of cell phones and email so rebellion was hard to organize. Anyone trying to do so by calling a public meeting risked falling into the crazies' hands, which as we've seen was something to be avoided. All that people could do was wait and hope that someone less crazy came along soon.

Lucky for them, German priest and theologian Martin Luther von Eisleben did come along, and he was quite a bit less crazy, although not altogether sane either. Despite his being two hundred years late, the minute I sensed he was ripe for change, I homed in like a bludger to a barbecue.

Marty was a Christian fundamentalist who insisted the Church should forget all about Indulgences and gluttony and sex before confession etc., but instead should go back to basics. Indeed he was so committed to this opinion that he would frequently rant and rave incoherently about it in the town square, which attracted a few dozen followers but mostly made him look like an idiot. Since no one was taking him seriously, I reminded him of what Saul and I had done on the road to Damascus, and suggested a repeat of that approach.

Together Marty and I wrote down his arguments in plain Latin, giving it the grandiose if not cumbersome title of *Disputatio Pro Declaratione Virtutis Indulgentiarum,* which soon got dubbed *the Ninety-Five Theses on the Power and Efficacy of Indulgences,* and later thankfully shortened to *The Ninety-Five Theses.*

This impressive sounding document was essentially an almanac and guide to encourage church leaders to lead dull lives, which Marty thought everyone should be doing anyway. His idea of a really good time was sitting around with a bunch of like-minded priests debating whether women were humans or not (hence my earlier comment about his dubious sanity).

This time-honoured hatred of women, incidentally, has permeated down the male line ever since *Homo* got *Erectus,* and surely underpins my extraordinary personal success. Just why men hate women so much is a story in itself that could fill volumes, but I feel I should tell a tiny bit of it since I have been an intimate observer and beneficiary of its evolution through time. The short version is: *you always hate what you're addicted to,* but the long version is a lot more involved. Female readers already know the story intuitively, so I won't be offended if they jump ten or so pages and pick up the story at *Ladies: this is where you tune back in.*

To explain man's hatred of women, I have to take you back a million years or so. It all started back in Chad when food became scarce in one section of the jungle that was surrounded on all sides by rivers. Any primates who could cross the river to more bountiful parts of the jungle stood a good chance of surviving; the rest starved or drowned and are thus no longer important to the story, or to humankind.

Since four-legged primates then and now are clumsy swimmers and almost invariably drown unless they're taught properly, the ones that could walk across shallower sections did better than those that tried to swim, and the ones that carried their babies across did even better. But to accomplish either feat meant waddling upright as best they could to hold their heads, and their babies' heads above water level. Very few primates could do this back then, but a few could, and a few were enough. The ones that could, got across and started eating better and making babies that could do the same trick.

Over the years it turned out that walking upright had other advantages, such as freeing up hands to collect more food than mouths could hold (ask any squirrel if you don't believe that's an advantage) so after a while the bipedal swagger really caught on. But in the great waterbed of life, an advantage can mean a disadvantage there.

Walking upright all the time was great for almost everything, but it put male noses on the wrong level for sniffing female backsides, which up until then had been essential for telling who was on heat and who wasn't. This nose-to-ass divergence severely flummoxed male chemistry, which now had no olfactory clues as to when it should deploy scarce inner resources to make sperm. Of course it didn't stop males practicing on any females who bent over to pick up a flower – that hadn't changed – but the few males who made sperm 24/7 scored more successful hits than those that couldn't.

This started a process of natural selection that meant any ensuing baby boys who inherited the continuous sperm-making trick were the ones more likely to grow up and make more of themselves, and so on. This explains why all (non-castrated) men reading this book are also making sperm. Who says they can't multi-task?

Now Raak had been one of those little baby boys, and when he grew up he and Muktuk had an understanding between them. He would rape her whenever he felt like it, and she would put up with it. Why? Because he was bigger and stronger than she was, so she couldn't stop him. Again, why? Because males then, like now, were lazy. It was much easier to catch smaller, weaker females than bigger, stronger ones. Natural selection did the rest, which explains the size imbalance between men and women today, on average.

These were tough and violent times for females – a situation that has seen only minor improvement in the intervening million years. When it comes to making babies, women still get a raw deal. The work isn't split even close to 50-50. Males have a single-minded commitment to the pleasurable business of delivering the plans to the factory, but once delivered their interest in the production and maintenance phase varies widely, with many men playing little or no significant part. Women have always been the dominant force in propagation, and for that they get royally screwed in more ways than one. Women have to work hard at making people; while the hardest thing men have do is try being better delivery boys.

And that's how things worked for hunter-gatherers for about a million years. From evolution's point of view (though not the female's) the process worked well and numbers grew. But because numbers grew, food got even harder to come by. Everyone was constantly on the move looking for it.

Nomads are typically too occupied with hunting and gathering to own anything substantial because they'd have to carry it everywhere they go. Carrying extraneous stuff around was too much of a drag so people learned to share everything to survive, with each member dependent on all the others. Indeed even offspring were raised as much by other females in the clan as by the mother.

Then things got complicated.

Brains got bigger than they really needed to be, and intelligence began filling the available space. People started having good ideas that resulted in a surplus of food being available, a bit like Sharmah's mammoth-trap, but a hundred thousand years earlier.

A food surplus brought its own set of new problems, like who should carry it and guard it and distribute it and so on. The extra food thus led to the completely new concept of ownership, and with ownership came the inevitable problem that someone would end up owning more than someone else. Thus private wealth was invented.

Then females began to notice that some males were better than others at accumulating wealth, so naturally they were attracted to them as a reliable source of nourishment for themselves and their offspring. Males were OK with this idea because it meant they got sex every night without having to sneak up and grab it from behind, which made it less strenuous and more leisurely on that account, again appealing to their inherent laziness. Sex for fun was born.

In fact it was so much fun that eventually males and females applied the concept of ownership to each other. Males owned their females, and females owned their males, and both got a bit annoyed when someone came sniffing around wanting a bit of the other. Jealously was thus invented to fend off would-be interlopers.

It wasn't a perfect system however, and occasionally some big lunk would hump another man's woman, causing fights to break out, disrupting the harmony of the mob. This would seriously annoy the chief who had more important things to do than solve domestic disputes every few days, so he laid down the first tribal law ever laid down – that woman was the property of man, and if anyone tried to take one without the owner's permission, the chief would kick him in the nuts or impose some other suitable deterrent.

After that, everyone paired up and lived happily ever after – for about a day and a half – until a younger, sexier female came along wanting a piece of someone else's action.

Since males were now walking sperm factories addicted to the squirting thereof, a wayward male would be quite happy to oblige any loose gal behind the bike shed as long as she didn't tell. But sooner or later she would have to tell because the ensuing pregnancy was a dead giveaway and a touch awkward to explain regardless of original intentions.

As we've seen, in years to come this would lead to the concept of virgin birth, but at this stage of the game imagination hadn't developed the requisite sophistication for a story like that. Instead fierce arguments would break out about who did what to whom, and who should feed the baby and change its nappy and so on – much the same as today.

Again, the chief had to adjudicate. But an unbiased judgement was never on the cards given the surge of lust that swelled his own loins every time a new bit of fluff sauntered past in a leopard-skin loincloth, so he was already predisposed to the male side of any paternity case.

Since he was duty-bound to uphold his own laws; and given that his wife was standing right next to him glaring at the tent forming in his loincloth, the only explanation that preserved his self-esteem was that the little slut in question was somehow manipulating his penis with special radio waves or magic or some such. She was the one making it happen, not him. Obviously it was the girl's fault that his Willie was pointing skyward; not his. And by the same logic the girl's unwanted baby was certainly not the fault of the poor chap who'd knocked her up. He'd clearly been put under the same evil spell too, poor fella.

All this happened well before my time, but the reason I know it's true is that Madam Self Delusion told me. She's been around forever, and she was definitely there when this happened. She convinced the chief that when his penis stood to attention for his wife it was a clear demonstration of his superior strength and honourable intentions; but when it dented his loincloth for a younger temptress it was surely not his doing. The young witch was working her magic spell on him. And the best way to break a spell was to give it a damn good spanking.

This turned out to be a bad idea. Males quickly discovered to their surprise and uncomfortable delight that this approach actually strengthened the spell, and led to even more unwanted babies. Throwing women into volcanoes (after they'd done the dirty of course) worked a little better, but such practices could be hard work and time-consuming, especially as volcanoes were way up on top of mountains, and vulcanism had peaked three million years earlier anyway. Finding an active one was always problematic.

Eventually someone suggested female infanticide as a means of nipping the problem in the bud, and this gained wide acceptance throughout human male-dom for many centuries, and is still practiced today, though it has had no obvious effect on breaking the spell.

So I ask you, after all this trouble and strife in men's lives supposedly caused by women, how could hatred of women *not* have eventuated?

Once Madam Self Delusion explained all this, a lot of things that had been troubling me suddenly fell into place. For instance, I never understood why Sharmah wanted to stay back at the camp with the women. I'd have thought that if he hated women, he'd want to stay with the guys – that a million years of evolution would have programmed him to avoid evil women.

But it turns out misogyny isn't genetic; it's learned. Boys have to spend their formative years in the company of women-haters to properly acquire it.

Sharmah was a smelly little orphan who didn't live with one family long enough to acquire any such prejudices, largely because he was left handed, and no one liked the idea that he ate food with the same hand that wiped his backside. So he was shunned at many levels. After puberty he found sexual relief in either hand and virtually none in trying to chat up girls who wouldn't come near him. Consequently he never got to experience the repeated and soul-destroying rejections that other boys suffered at the whim of pernickety females.

But for boys who hung around older men for long periods (e.g. clergy in the Middle Ages) misogyny became an unquestionable paradigm. Absolute submission to the Church was paramount, and devoting any time to a wife simply wasn't on.

Celibacy was presented as *the* criterion for entry into monastic life; take it or leave it. The ones that took it hated it. No mater how hard they prayed, they just couldn't quell their earthy desires for women. Those with earthy desires for men instead, had a ready source of release on hand in every sense of the word, but those who fancied the fairer sex were frustrated to distraction.

Somehow demonic female radio waves were getting through even the thickest of monastic stonewalls, jerking the g-strings of their glandes to the point that eventually something had to be done – e*rgo:* witch hunts – the most systematic form of misogyny ever invented, which satisfied two primal urges roughly simultaneously, although the sex usually came before the slaughter; but not always.

I don't mean to pretend that women are entirely blameless in this process. Of course they aren't. Women too are driven by sex, and are fully aware of their innate power to subjugate men to the status of willing, unwitting slaves. But I've never seen that power wielded on a grand coordinated scale. Then again I've only been around for a million years, so there's probably still time. But the hurdle that females face is immense.

The problem here is that females don't cooperate well. They have a hardwired distrust of each other; frequently perceiving other females as pernicious rivals instead of potential collaborators. You'll know this distrust as jealousy, but it's really just a variant of primal fear, notably the fear of losing desirability and relevance as a propagator of humankind.

Desirability and relevance are both indispensable and formidable female drivers for propagating genes, and are not easily set aside simply for the pursuit of a greater good.

So despite any localised social uproar that jealousy creates for men on a day-to-day basis, men have little to fear from jealousy from an overall superiority perspective. Jealousy ensures that women will never organise into a formidable counter-force. This is what makes women the weaker sex, and the main reason men hold the upper hand (and position). It has nothing to do with muscles.

Ironically, jealousy is invoked in women by precisely the same thing that invokes sexual desire in men, i.e. the sight of an attractive female. Jealousy is therefore almost certainly a primeval chemical pattern like me, but much older, probably living in sin with Primal Fear deep in the amygdala. This surely explains why I've never been able to recruit jealousy directly in my quest for world domination, but lucky for me it has kept womankind in disarray, meaning I've only had to bend men to my purpose. The women have obediently tagged along, glaring at each other and calling each other witches in the process.

Even the myth of witches is a male invention designed to divide and conquer women who might otherwise pool their power. But it wasn't a deliberate invention; it was opportunistic. Nor was the opportunity caused by men; it was caused by the absence of men.

With so many men off fighting this war or that, or playing pirates at sea and whatnot, there were never enough decent men to go around. Women were frequently left to fend for themselves, becoming frustrated and inventive as a result.

Single and solitary women wishing to avoid unwanted pregnancies found it easier to survive living in or near forests, where they could hide from errant men afflicted by the midlife crisis. They could also forage for food there, and many new and interesting foods were discovered by forest-dwelling women prepared to risk death tasting this new herb or that new mushroom. But occasionally a woman would stumble upon an unknown hallucinogenic plant, which is where the witch myth begins.

Flying high on magic mushrooms or wild marihuana brought blissful relief to loneliness, and, quite sensibly, a woman who discovered such an effect would keep it secret to avoid being vulnerable under its influence. During such blissful intoxication, it wasn't uncommon to use a broomstick as a reminder of the pleasures their absent menfolk once gave them. Nor was it out of the question to try to magnify that pleasure with unctions and concoctions smeared along the broomstick's shaft or indeed at its tip.

But with so many undiscovered toxins lurking in unfamiliar plants, a risky experimentrix could easily die in the throes of ecstasy riding her broomstick, to be found days or weeks later, withered, wasted and hideous with a broomstick 'twixt her thighs. No wonder people made up stories.

Ladies: This is where you tune back in, but before we continue with Luther's exploits, may I offer this unsolicited opinion? As custodians of the human race I think you're doing a pretty mediocre job of it. It's no skin of my imaginary nose but if I thought for one moment that humans were working towards becoming more civilised I would be very disappointed at the female contribution to that end.

Having watched humans bumble along from one mess to the next it's pretty obvious that men are to blame for most of it – the evidence is simply overwhelming. But ladies, before you smugly agree, let me ask: where were you?

It's oft been said that behind every great man is a great woman. Well if that's true she's a bloody long way behind. Every murderous, torturing genocidal manic I've had the privilege to infect over the eons has always gone home to the wife at the end of the day for some tender loving reassurance that he's doing a good job; and she's given it. He fantasises that he's doing it all for her anyway, such is the way the male mind is wired up. Men don't do anything unless food or sex is the ultimate reward, and over the centuries women have been largely in charge of both. So I ask: ladies why not set him straight? Stop being so wimpy-weak.

Surely you know what your man gets up to while he's out? The blood on his shirt can't always be explained by clumsy shaving. Why don't you speak up? Why don't you tell him to stop? Why don't you make him stop? Withdraw your services until he does. You have a thousand times more power than you realise. I know Madman Self Delusion is strong in you but how do you let her get away with murder? And I'm not talking figuratively.

I was inside the wives and girlfriends of the Nazi Holocaust torturers (to pick one example of thousands). When their menfolk came home for dinner after a full day on the gas ovens, or down in the dungeons hammering sharp German nails through bleeding Polish fingernails; the ladies all knew what was going on. I could tell it violated everything decent in them; yet they said nothing; did nothing. They had nice houses and clean clothes and good food on the table. It was all they wanted to think about. Shame on them. Shame on you.

Then again, it's your species not mine; I suppose you can do what you like with it.

So, back to Martin Luther and his contribution to me. If you and I bothered to read his *Ninety-Five Theses* today, we'd find it pretty small beer; but back in Marty's day it was a knife to the throat of Catholic commercialism. It denounced Indulgency transactions as un-Christian, and thus threatened the Church's principal income stream. Moreover it claimed that the only thing Indulgences actually did was propagate greed and promiscuity, and did nothing for your chances of getting into heaven. It also tried to deny existing and future popes the right to grant pardons on my behalf, which really scraped a raw nerve in the ego of the then-reigning pope, Pope Leo X. Yet as bad as all that was, I'm sure it could have been worked out by civilised discussion and negotiation if Marty hadn't twisted the knife by calling Leo an antichrist! Yes an antichrist! That's as insulting as it gets in Christendom.

Well, as they say: *them's fight'n words*. Leo summoned Marty to the German town of Worms to attend a special Papal meeting called a Diet, at which he planned to make Marty eat his words, and force him to accept the Diet of Worms.

English readers can be forgiven for thinking this is a clumsy food joke on my part, but I swear to me that it's all true (look it up if you don't believe).

At the Diet of Worms, Leo reminded Marty in crystal clear Latin, that a hundred years earlier Pope Alexander V had barbecued the heretic Jan Hus alive until he wasn't, for saying similarly unpopular things about Indulgences. The clear implication was that Marty should mind his manners lest he himself be similarly immolated; or at the very least lose vital bodily appendages at Leo's whim.

Tough talk I agree, but Marty was even tougher, and suggested Leo go fuck himself. Marty was therefore instantly excommunicated; but as we'll see in a moment, in a huge tactical error on Leo's part he didn't roast Marty immediately; or ever.

Inquisitions had been running non-stop for three hundred years by then and were essentially the Vatican's clumsy approach to genocide, targeting not ethnicity, but rival religions, women and disobedient people in authority.

Lucky for Marty he'd chosen to be disobedient in Germany. If he'd chosen to be a disobedient in Spain, I probably wouldn't remember him, and you certainly wouldn't have heard of him, although the residents of

Cordoba would have surely heard him screaming for a week or so. But Marty never went to Spain, so the Spanish Inquisition passed him by. It did, however, come perilously close.

You see Marty's ongoing survival was never part of Leo's original plan. Despite Leo's public assurances that Marty would not be harmed at the Diet, the lying pope had secretly arranged to have Marty tortured to death in the most heinous ways he could imagine; and believe me this pope could imagine some pretty heinous ways.

I was inside Leo's head of course, so I got a torturer's-ear recital of the screams he was eagerly anticipating; and even if his imagination faltered there was an official Papal Mangler's Manual to refer to for inspiration. Either way, I could tell he was pretty keen to get started.

But as things turned out, Leo never got a chance to try out his favourite screamers on Marty because the Great Random intervened, choosing to drop yet another cloud of Black Death on Germany just in the nick of time. This sent Leo running for cover back home to Rome, where other issues distracted him so much that Marty got a chance to get organised. Nice one, Random.

So, excommunicated *and* alive, Marty was now free to engage in some indulgences of his own by starting a new strain of me. I was so jubilant at the prospect that I let him call his new religion whatever he wanted to. I thought *Lutherans* was a bit dull, but that was Marty all over. What I did love however, was the unexpected consequence of his excommunication.

You see Marty wasn't the only person in Europe who was fed up with the pope. A lot of important folks in Germany, Czechoslovakia, Hungary, France, England, Holland and pretty much everywhere in Christendom were also fed up with absolute Papal power making the Vatican rich, and their lives miserable. But they'd been too scared to do anything about it, lest they themselves be excommunicated.

The e-word invariably struck terror in the hearts and souls of Catholics; but like many fears in life, the fear was steeped in the word as much as the deed. As Marty had shown, provided you could avoid becoming a well-done steak at the stake, excommunication wasn't all that bad, and not much worse than being kicked out of a club you didn't like anyway. A lightning bolt didn't zap you in the back or anything like that; so if Marty could cope then so could they.

Six heavyweight princes with the imposing names of: Elector, John the Steadfast; Margrave George of Brandenburg; Ernest I the Confessor and Duke of Brunswick Lunenburg & Celle; Landgrave Philip of Hesse; Francis Duke of Brunswick & Lunenburg-Gifhorn; and Prince Wolfgang of Anhalt-Köthen all got together and wrote a letter to Leo protesting at the way Catholic laws were being dreamed up in Rome to suit the Vatican, without taking account of their wider princely views.

Despite these princes being well respected in their countries, and rather powerful in their own right, Leo just told them all to fuck off (not his exact words, but close enough) and publicly declared that he wouldn't even read their letter, which he damned as being a *Protestant Letter*.

A lesson for all those giddy with power: never give your enemy a catchy name, especially when they can afford a barrel of ink and a printing press as recently invented by Marty's fellow countryman Johannes Gutenberg.

These *Protestants*, as Leo kept calling them, made multiple copies of their letter and pinned them up all over Europe to help the average man in the street understand what a nasty piece of work Leo really was.

Naturally Leo was livid at this overt display of disloyalty but he had to wait in hiding until the plague lifted before he could take his revenge. When the plague finally eased, Leo was literally itching to dispatch Marty once and for all, and he set about assembling evidence and equipment for the mother of all excommunications. It was going to be an historic event guaranteed to quell disobedience forever. He even purchased an elephant for the occasion, though I never worked out what he planned to do with it.

But in one of the greatest ironic twists in all of recorded history, Leo's itching turned out to be as much about mosquito bites as vengeance, and the scratching pope died of malaria before issuing invitations.

Nice one, Random. From that day on, in Europe anyway, Catholicism started to slip down the Vatican gargoyles.

Marty really belted the piñata when he started Lutheranism, and he kick-started an avalanche that hasn't stopped yet.

Suddenly all sorts of *isms* were popping up alongside Lutheranism, such as Anglicanism, Anabaptism, Reformism, Congregationalism (a real mouthful), Calvinism, Presbyterianism, and Pietism; followed later by some *ists*, like Methodists, Adventists, Separatists, Baptists and Puritanists and on and on and on; all vying for a piece of the obedience market.

At last count there were twenty thousand different strains of me in the United States alone, which reminds me of the day that tax advisers were deregulated; suddenly there was one on every street corner.

You might think I would be sad at this eventuality – that loss of faith in my God-me version would dilute my life's purpose – but I had already concluded by now that diversity was a good thing, so I wasn't worried. But there was one *ism* still to come that forced me to rethink my whole *raison d'etre;* and I'm still readjusting to it.

13

CHARLIE AND THE INSANITY FACTORY

If my unwitting typist has followed my instructions properly, the publisher's page in the front of this book should show it was first published in 2014 AD, which by coincidence is fourteen hundred years, or two seven hundred year cycles since I answered Muhammad's desperate prayer. Interestingly fourteen hundred also turns out to be a significant number in the evolution of human gullibility.

It took about fourteen hundred years for Christianity to reach its peak of brutality in the Inquisitions then slowly taper off. The last of the Catholic Inquisitions (so far) didn't end until as late as the mid 1800's when it wrecked the life of a little boy by forcibly taking him from his Jewish parents to make him Catholic. Now that Islam is celebrating its fourteen-hundredth birthday, Muslims too are finding more and more inventive ways to wreck lives and kill people they don't like, or even know. If Islam follows the same pattern, I expect Muslim Muftis and Mullahs to continue their imperfect version of do-or-die religious conversion for another four hundred years or so before petering out. By the same logic Islamic carnage should now be at its peak. Yet it hasn't come even close to reaching the screaming heights of the Catholic Inquisitions. And although it has four hundred more years to run, I'm not convinced it's going to make it. Here's why.

While Catholicism thrived on a successful policy of threatening to kill people if they didn't sign up, Islam (my latest version of it anyway) seems to have missed this crucial step, and has developed a self defeating mutation of just killing for killing's sake. Infidels aren't being offered the choice to convert as a way of avoiding being blown up on the spot. They are simply being blown up on the spot for no apparent purpose. Indeed this mutation has gone so cancerous that Sunnis and Shiites now kill each other just so they can watch the fireworks; and will even kill themselves when they catch the rare, suicide strain. As spectacular as all this is, none of it is useful to me.

I saw something like this happen in England around the time of Martin Luther, when King Henry VIII was having his famous religious doubts. I don't mean he was having doubts about God-me or Jesus-me – he was absolutely devoted in that regard. No, his doubts were about whether popes were really my true representatives on earth.

For years Henry had been brown-nosing Pope Leo to reserve a spot in heaven fit for a king, and Leo honestly considered Henry to be the apple of his eye; his most devoted subject. In truth they were good mates, and Leo told Henry it was as good as done.

Then Henry started having marital problems and it all started to go bad. To make matters worse, Pope Leo up and died of malaria while organising Luther's demise, so the promise of an everlasting deckchair for Henry was looking a bit shaky.

Leo was then succeeded by a German pope, Pope Adrian VI, who'd never heard of Henry and didn't really know where Rome was either, since he'd been elected *in absentia* by Vatican powerbrokers expecting him to be their puppet. Henry was now rightfully worried.

Well, as you should know by now: power goes to everyone's head. The new Pope Adrian publicly announced that Germans don't make good puppets (well they do actually, but only the wooden ones) and he certainly wasn't going to dangle at the end of any Roman strings.

I was busy with Martin Luther's new church at the time, so I missed the Catholic shenanigans that ensued, but I think you can guess what happened next. The perfectly fit and healthy Pope Adrian suddenly and mysteriously died within a few months of showing his hand, and a new, more cooperative pope was elected by the Vatican mafia. That's got to be a lesson worth learning: if you're planning to be awkward, there's no need to crow about it.

The pope they elected was Pope Clement VII who definitely knew Henry and didn't like him one bit. Henry now realised his heavenly penthouse was going to be leased to someone else. Moreover his marital problems had deteriorated to their frustrating worst.

Marriage, eh! What can you do?

You see Henry was married to Catherine, a pious and exceedingly dull Catholic Spanish Princess; but Henry wanted to have sex with a fun-loving bit of local fluff called Anne Boleyn whom he'd noticed flitting about at Court. She'd been tugging at his regal Willie with her magic radio waves ever since Catherine stopped transmitting, but Anne had made it clear to Henry that he wasn't allowed to touch her crystal set unless he married her first.

These folks weren't in the jungles of Chad nor were they wearing leopard-skin loin cloths, but I think you get my drift; nothing much had changed inside men's heads for the past million years. But outside men's heads things had changed quite a lot. Society now had rules; rules about marriage and divorce and all that wet blanket stuff that got in the way of randy kings wanting to have a good time; rules that Henry decided to change. Well, he was the king after all. Kings make the rules, don't they? So kings can change the rules, can't they? Henry certainly thought so.

Being a good, albeit temporary Catholic, Henry wrote to Clement as a matter of courtesy to explain that Catherine was as dull as dishwater in bed, and only made baby girls if she consented to make them at all, which was no use to a king in need of a male successor. He was going to ditch Catherine for Anne, who was a far better prospect for making the sons he needed to continue his kingly privileges down the male bloodline.

The problem was that Clement reckoned popes were bigger than kings, and thus made bigger rules. Moreover, Catherine was a good Catholic from Spanish royalty whence Clement drew significant Indulgences. And since Spain was the operational headquarters of the Inquisition anyway, Clement figured he had plenty of good reasons to deny Henry permission to divorce Catherine. Instead he recommended marriage guidance therapy, and presented Henry with a hefty Indulgency fine for having such un-Catholic thoughts.

Well that just made Henry hopping mad.

Henry hadn't been asking for permission; he was simply trying to set the pope straight on who made the rules in England. In fact it made him so hopping mad he took a leaf out of Marty's book and set up his own religion in competition, which he called his Church of England, with himself as its Earthly head answerable directly to me in heaven.

I didn't mind of course, since he was adamant about spreading me about; but it did mean I'd have to redraw the org-chart yet again, which was starting to get a bit tedious. Reorganisations are such a distraction.

Well, to make everything fit together properly, Henry set about destroying Catholic cathedrals, churches, bibles and beliefs everywhere in England; and he declared open season on priests and practising Catholics as a way of boosting support for his own particular version of Protestantism.

But Henry (and I'm finally getting close to my point now) always gave accused Catholics the option of changing religions to avoid the chopping block. He could see the obvious downside of killing taxpayers without at least offering them the chance to remain alive, and thus remain taxpayers.

I was in there of course advising everybody to switch sides to stay alive; and I did a pretty good job too given that the UK is still brimming with of Anglicans, my recent Islamic infiltration notwithstanding.

Which finally brings me to my point in the present day: the current Muslim mayhem that is distracting the modern world is completely at odds with Henry's highly successful strategy of religious conversion. My modern Islam version seems to have skipped the crucial step of offering potential victims the chance to convert, and instead just kills them for the fun of hearing the bang. This crucial oversight will surely prove to be its downfall, since killing potential converts is obviously suicidal to the cause.

If this isn't obvious and you need evidence, just go back a few years to Algeria in February 2002, where it was spectacularly demonstrated – albeit on a small scale – by one of that country's over-zealous Islamic leaders of the Armed Islamic Group – a rebel who called himself Abou Talha Antar, although his real name was Antar Zouabri. I wish people wouldn't do that.

Zouabri concluded from his own strict interpretation of the Koran that the only pure form of Islam possible was the particular one he carried around inside his head. Everyone else's interpretations were therefore impure forms that had to be cleansed.

Since *everyone else* included the entire population of Algeria, he set about that task by shooting anyone he could point his machine gun at. Predictably the first to go were his faithful and somewhat surprised followers. When they were all dead, he started shooting all life-forms within range until he ran out of ammo, whereupon a few survivors that were still ammo'ed up, shot him.

You won't remember Zouabri. The incident went almost unreported at the time given the larger uproar following Bush-the-Dopier's reaction to 9/11 – which was to bomb countries that weren't responsible, and imprison anyone with a black beard regardless of gender.

(Funny story: Despite the state-of-the-art navigational resources available to President Bush and his super-arsenal, he in fact attacked the wrong country, missing the offending country of Afghanistan by a whole other country, and bombed Iraq instead. The in-between country of Iran is still thanking its lucky stars that American geography classes don't involve world atlases.)

But back to Zouabri's antics, the only reason I mention them at all is because they hint at where today's misguided Islam might be headed if someone doesn't twig that killing everyone is a poor strategy for spreading me about.

I, for one, am very disappointed at this odd development, especially given all the work that Mo and I put into spreading Allah-me throughout the world. And I know that Mo would be devastated if he ever found out; which of course he won't because he's dead. But even if he wasn't he certainly wouldn't recognise the Islam of today.

Still, plenty of other me-versions have died out over the millennia due to bad local management, so I won't be shedding any tears, not that I could. There are plenty of would-be Mo replacements waiting in the wings, but sadly no blockbuster heavenly signs have arisen with which to wow them, so I haven't managed to get one pumped into a frenzy yet. But I'm keeping watch.

For completeness – since I mentioned it at the beginning of the chapter – the last officially recorded act of the Catholic Inquisitions occurred surprisingly recently in 1858, while your great great grandmother was probably alive. Here's what happened:

Priests acting for Pope Pius IX decided to abduct six-year-old Edgardo Mortara, a Jewish boy living with his family in Bologna, a town in the middle of what you now call Italy. It's a strange little tale with an uncomfortable air of paedophilia hanging over it, though none was ever proved.

Edgardo's twelve-year-old nanny told her priest that she had secretly baptised the boy while she was bathing him, to save him from Judaism – which every good Catholic knew was the heinous organization that had killed Jesus. Apparently she hadn't read the Talmud either.

Just how a twelve-year-old girl could perform the exclusively priestly sacrament of baptism was never explained, but the priest saw it as a way of making a name for himself. He passed the girl's vital piece of national intelligence onto the Vatican, whereupon Pius despatched a team of armed henchmen to steal Edgardo from his family.

Despite little Edgardo's parents' appeal for police help and court justice, Edgardo was taken and remained a lifelong captive of the pope, and was even brainwashed during his all-important formative years into becoming a Catholic priest. How's that for a viral success story?

Meanwhile the international outcries over the kidnapping, which poured into Rome from every state of Europe and America, rolled off Pius's back like tears on crocodile hide. Indeed Pius was so sure of himself that he told a goodly number of foreign diplomats, statesmen and the occasional sovereign representative to fuck off out of Rome and quit bothering him with their whiney protests. He was proud of what he'd done. The boy was his, and that was that.

Well as they say, pride cometh before the fall. Pius's contempt of all matters moral, legal and decent motivated the disparate Italian states to rally together into a unified nation so they could drive rampant papal power back into its dark crypt where it couldn't damage so many innocent lives. So if you've ever wondered why Vatican City is so tiny compared to the rest of the Italian peninsular that popes once considered their own, you can thank little Edgardo for being the catalyst.

While Edgardo's abduction was the last officially recorded act of Catholic Inquisitors, it wasn't the last example of the carnage that ordinary people were delighted to inflict on others when someone in authority said it was right and good to do so.

In recent times the likes of Robespierre, Hitler, PolPot, Hirohito, Ceauşescu, Stalin, Talaat, Enver, Djemal, Zedong, Milosevic, Truman, Kennedy, Khomeini, Gadafi, Hussein and a couple of Bushes have all given ordinary people the green light to murder and/or torture with impunity. And people being what you are – hardly anyone refused.

Indeed, sometimes, like in Africa, it didn't even require a green light from authority. All it took was a container-full of Mikhail Kalashnikov's favourite invention – his now ubiquitous Avtomat Kalashnikova model 1947 to be left unattended. Mix sexually frustrated young men with unlimited AK47s, and the shooting will start automatically – spontaneous human combustion you might say. But as long as everyone knows they're going to die one day, what do I care? I'm just a thought, remember?

Given the highly predictable appearance of new versions of me every seven hundred years or so, and the new heights of brutality we can expect to be carried out in my name in times to come, I can't help looking to the future. As we've seen already in 1571 Martin Luther gave me the latest opportunity to mutate significantly. Basic arithmetic will tell you that 1571 AD plus 700 equals 2271 AD, which hasn't happened yet, so you might think a mutation is too early to think about. But given the wide error band in my seven hundred year cycle, another strain might have popped up and we just haven't noticed.

Sure, there have been plenty of minor variants such as the *isms* and *ists* I mentioned at the end of the previous chapter, but nothing startlingly different enough to call a genuine mutation, so it's tempting to say there hasn't been one yet.

Or has there?

Well, yes there has, but it came in such an odd form you might not have recognized it. And I'm not talking about the one I hinted at back in Sharmah's day, when the boys were trying to impress the girls by kicking caribou bladders around.

Sport isn't a religion yet, and I've had nothing to do with its burgeoning popularity. It doesn't have its roots in my original idea that people are going to die one day, so I can't claim credit. Nor can I get a decent grip on the concept; but I am keeping a close eye on it just the same.

It certainly has the early appearances of a religion. Its congregations meet on Saturdays and Sundays; they worship their idols as gods; their tunics and paraphernalia are rife with icons and symbols; and (the definitive characteristic for any religion) when a group chooses to be offended by another group, it encourages hatred and condones violence towards its rivals.

Sports fans could easily be mistaken for the *nuveaux faithful* because they exhibit nearly identical behaviours to their counterparts concurrently worshiping in churches, mosques synagogues and temples, all aiming to reinforce the belief that they are right and everyone else is wrong. But sport doesn't have a supreme being to guide it, and therein lays the difference: there's no *me* at the top.

Despite this, I watch for behavioural signs that someone – a human perhaps or a rival thought pattern – might try to claim that vacant throne. The Pharaohs did it once; it might again be possible for someone to hijack the very characteristics that I myself need to propagate.

All it would take is a sociopathic authority figure – a shock-jock radio announcer perhaps or a well-worshiped rock star to incite fans into murdering opposition teams in his name or in the noble cause of team supremacy. With modern tools like Facebook and Twitter at Madam Self Delusion's disposal, such a cult following would surely grow into a religion quite rapidly.

If that were to happen, the most deplorable aspects of humanity that I rely on for my fun could suddenly be denied me, and I would have to find a way to counter it, possibly by turning all sports into an evil that loyal me-believers would feel duty-bound to destroy. But it hasn't happened yet, so I continue to keep a close watch. After all, I have to do something to while away the eons.

Well if sport with its close behavioural analogies to religion isn't the new mutation, then you'll be asking: what is?

Look around at humans today and you can easily divide them into two broad categories – the ones who say they believe in one of my many forms, and the ones who say they don't. This is a relatively new phenomenon.

Before 1859, while not everyone fell into the first category, the vast majority did, and virtually everyone *said* they believed in a god of some sort because to imply otherwise was socially unwise. It was hard, for example, to get a good table at a restaurant if you booked it as A. N. Atheist, 666 Apostate Lane, Purgatory-on-Hades. It simply wasn't done.

Back then it was just too weird to even imply that you didn't believe in me. Entire nations had grown up on the mantra that I was in my heaven and all was right with the world. To question this, as we've seen time and time again, was to risk tasting death in one of its many bitter flavours.

Then something peculiar happened in 1859 that changed all that forever and perhaps even made me a better thought.

For most of his early life, a wealthy but sickly English kid called Charles Darwin believed in me at both levels. Firstly he knew he was going to die one day because he'd seen lots of other people do it, and had studied quite a bit of science to be able to prove it. As a biologist, he was well aware that life was a sexually transmitted peculiarity of matter that ultimately led to its own demise. In this regard he believed in me completely.

Secondly he fully believed that I was his particular God, which misconception I had perpetuated rather efficiently down the European line of humanity since Luther and I worked together. French, German, Spanish and English Kings infected with one or other of my strains had done a bang-up job of ensuring all their subjects would at least *claim* to believe in me, even if deep down they weren't sure. By the nineteen century my myth was so virulent that I didn't even have to work at it to get myself spread around.

My Anglican Jesus strain was so powerful in nineteenth century England thanks to Henry VIII, that Charles Darwin got fully infected via his parents in the first years of his life, with virtually no direct intervention from me. Indeed Charlie even entered Cambridge University to study theology with the intention of becoming one of my foot soldiers. Furthermore his seemingly unassailable belief in me was reinforced daily (and nightly but that's another story) by his profoundly religious cousin Emma with whom he spent a great deal of time and eventually married. Thus it came as a bit of a shock when he began to drift.

Despite his faith and apparent commitment to me, Charlie was a troubled character; I sensed it as soon as he began studying dog breeding. Dogs by the way are the absolute bane of my life. Everyone loves them and breeds them like rabbits, which is OK for a while. But then they start tinkering with dog variability, deliberately selecting puppies that appeal most, and then breeding those together to make more adorable little ones, and so on. Pretty soon they've made such different looking dogs to the ones they started with, that they reckon they're God myself. What impertinence!

Charlie was one of those people, but he didn't just confine his meddling to dogs. He tinkered with all sorts of animals and plants such as orchids, grasses, birds, peas, pigeons, mussels, fish, and to some extent even his own children, observing how one child had acquired his characteristics while another had acquired his wife's.

And he didn't confine his tinkering to living creatures. He studied fossils and noticed how much they looked like living animals, only sometimes much bigger or much smaller, which didn't really jell with the longstanding, though strange in my opinion, notion that I had made everything to stay the same forever.

This strange notion that the animals of the day were identical to those that strolled off Noah's Ark was called the Stability of Species and had been around for a very long. I was around when it arose but it had nothing to do with me.

Four thousand years before Charlie came on the scene, a Greek chap called Aristotle pretended it was true simply because he was a bit of a sook and didn't want his cushy life to ever change, so he made up the idea all by himself, imagining that if he believed it hard enough then it would be true.

At the time I thought he was joking since changes to the world had been so massive over time that they ought to have been obvious to anyone who cared to look. But I forgot that when Aristotle made up the Stability of Species hypothesis, I'd been around for a million years while he'd been around for about thirty. Change was obvious to me, but virtually invisible to him.

If I'd been paying attention I would have realised he was serious, and I'd have suggested it was a silly idea that would surely bite someone in the bum one day. But once I realised he actually believed it, and that it wasn't interfering with my work, I simply let dreamers be dreamers, and assumed it would go the way of the Flat Earth hypothesis.

But over the centuries the Stability of Species grew into something really quite absurd, with supposedly learned men of the times looking for more and more reasons why it had to be true in the face of more and more evidence that it clearly wasn't.

At one stage of the proceedings someone even proposed that I had created Man in my own image, and that was the reason why men (and presumably women one rung lower down) still looked like Adam and Eve. They were immutable and securely positioned at the top of the food chain. I rather liked the idea that I might have a physical appearance so I let it ride, expecting that even a half-wit would realise it couldn't possibly be true. Why?

Well, given that there were about a billion people on Earth back then, and, save for identical twins, they all looked quite different to each other. Could everyone somehow convince themselves they all looked like me? I didn't get it, and still don't.

How could a three-month-old Chinese boy from Manchuria and an eighty-year-old Hillbilly woman from the Ozarks both look like me? I mean, what the hell did they think I looked like anyway? You'd think someone would have twigged that I couldn't possibly look like a billion different people all at the same time.

Maybe they thought I was a mirror? That might have explained at least part of it, but I don't recall anyone mentioning mirrors as an explanation for such a loopy idea. Yet everyone seemed utterly convinced of it right up until the nineteenth century, by which time I'd realised that Madam Self Delusion had been up to her old shenanigans again, so I let her have her fun.

Even when Charlie started questioning things, at first I didn't think much would come of it; a few curiosities here; a readjustment to geological time there, a new comet perhaps, but nothing earth shattering.

But then he went on that cruise; that damned five-year cruise on the Beagle, which was supposed to re-map the South American coastline. Boring! I assumed he was going as an assistant cartographer or something; I never imagined he would re-map the entire plant and animal kingdoms instead. Even when I caught him packing his microscope and notebook I wasn't worried. I figured it was more for hobby reasons and certainly not for serious investigation. And he wasn't even going to be paid for the work he did, if you can believe it? I mean who takes a job for five years without getting paid? Isn't that called slavery?

Well five years was a long time to sit on a rocky boat and think, even if he was seasick for most of it. But time, he realised, was the vital ingredient to everything in life. Time was the key to complexity. It was the element that people ignored when they beheld the staggering intricacy of living things, like eyes, and hands and bee swarms and flying bats and flightless birds.

The problem was that people never stopped to imagine what could happen given enough time. This wasn't surprising, since people can't grasp time very well and certainly don't give a hoot about anything before or after their own lifetimes. Moreover back then they believed Man was the great mover and shaker of everything on the planet, which misconception had been instilled upon them by the enormous power at their fingertips brought about by the Industrial Revolution. They'd pretty well convinced themselves that if a human being couldn't do something then it probably wasn't possible for it to be done at all, my mysterious ways notwithstanding.

But on the Beagle, Charlie had plenty of time. Time allowed his ploddingly slow, methodical, inexorable logic to chip away at all the aspects of the world that had hitherto been attributed to me and me alone. Things like the colours of flowers, and perfectly hexagonal honeycombs, and birds' songs, and peacocks' fans and fishes' eyes and just about everything you see when you look outdoors.

Now I was forced to take interest. This was *my* territory. These were the beauties and wonders of the world that had only ever been explained by my having created them – things that were so elegantly designed and presented, that up until now no one had had the gall to question my obvious hand in their design. The mysteries of the world had always been held up as rock-solid, in-your-face, can't-deny-it evidence of yours truly. I certainly didn't need some upstart of a failed vicar sowing the seeds of doubt in loyal English minds.

Fifty years earlier Charlie would have been burned at the stake for a heck of a lot less insolence than this; but England had since outlawed such practices, and try as I might, I couldn't find a single soul to strike a match on my behalf. Bugger! This was unprecedented! The threat of torture and death were my favoured persuasions. Were people becoming civilised at last? Surely not.

Without primal fear to assist, the only weapons I had left were ridicule and sex, which weren't nearly as effective. Nevertheless I persisted with them. I nudged

Charlie's peers to ridicule both he and his work at every opportunity. But he was of such good temperament that ridicule simply rolled off him like water off a duck's back. Worse still it actually made him work harder to convince his critics he was right. Simultaneously I tweaked Mrs. Darwin's fears by reminding her again and again that Charlie was doomed to burn in hell if he continued with his evolutionary nonsense. I even insisted she withhold sexual favours from him, but she was too randy and too loyal a wife to keep her legs together for long. She even pumped out a few more little Darwins to add insult to injury.

What the hell was happening? Was I losing my grip? Was this the end? I didn't understand it. People weren't doing my bidding on autopilot anymore. The little blighters were thinking for themselves.

Thinking wasn't new of course, but these folks were thinking at a whole different level. People had been thinking since before Abram was a boy, but they confined their thinking to eking-out a living; to figuring out when to plant crops; that summer always returned despite the ferocity of winter; that sex really did make babies despite the bonk-to-birth time lag, and so on. That kind of thinking was OK. People needed a little bit of knowledge, otherwise they'd have stayed in the trees like Raak and Muktuk, and I wouldn't have had such complex minds to mess with.

But it was essential that people remained ignorant of the majority of what they saw. Curiosity was always a nagging problem of course. I hadn't been able to do much about curiosity because Muktuk had passed her hardwired curiosity into her kids. Nevertheless it was a constant irritation. Every new thing that people encountered was like a chipped tooth to a tongue; they just wouldn't leave it alone.

Someone's kid would always ask, 'Daddy, where does lightning come from?' Or, 'Mommy, why is the sky blue?' Or 'Where does the sun go at night?'

I couldn't stop them asking, but I was always there first, ready to help out. Before they had a chance to sit down and try to work out such problems, I would provide an instant explanation that was easy to remember so they wouldn't have to admit they didn't know. I told them that I was the creator of everything mysterious and unknown. I made everything happen; they needn't trouble their little minds about it. As we've seen earlier, they would always latch onto the first explanation they heard because it filled the space nicely and avoided deeper contemplation.

Early on in the game I found such explanations worked better if I gave people a little shot of a feel-good drug like serotonin or oxytocin. Then they would just love whatever explanation I gave them and they would declare it to be correct for evermore.

My motto has always been: *What satisfies; clarifies*, and since satisfaction is nothing more than a chemical dropped in the right place at the right time (a task to which I am well suited) I could make people believe almost anything I wanted. Indeed they loved the drugs so much they became addicted and would attack anyone who sought to interrupt the flow.

Anyone questioning my simple, feel-good explanations was a bounder and a killjoy bent on killing their joy. Killing a killjoy made perfect sense to them – the way killing a drug cop makes perfect sense to a drug pusher. The body count through history should prove this to even the most sceptical denier. You can see that, can't you? You're smart enough to see that. You're very smart, I can tell. Of course you are. You're way smarter than most people. Mm, feel that? It was a little shot of something nice I just gave you.

So you can imagine how I kicked myself for not picking up that Charlie was different. Maybe it was because he wasn't thinking about just lightning, or sky colour, or even the properties of light, he was thinking about EVERYTHING! The whole shebang! The grand explanation of life itself! This was a whole new ballgame and I simply wasn't prepared for it. Many philosophers in the past had tinkered with it, from Aristotle to Zubiri, but no one had attacked it as seriously and methodically as Charlie. Why?

Because no one had taken five years off work to think about it.

Curse that cruise. If Charlie had stayed home I could have distracted him with food and sex and family squabbles and his recurring mental illness and politics and any number of things under my control. But away out at sea on a piddly little ninety-foot by twenty-five-foot brig-sloop like Her Majesty's Ship *Beagle*, what could I distract him with?

The best I could manage at short notice was a rip-roaring argument with his suicidal captain, Robert Fitzroy on the subject of slavery, a concept which Fitzroy agreed with, and Charlie abhorred. It was a perfect, irreconcilable subject for a long argument on a long cruise. But damn all civilised Brits; they kissed and made up (not literally I hasten to add) and simply agreed to disagree, getting on with each other just fine for the rest of the voyage.

And Darwin wouldn't have even been on the damn boat except for a touch of madness that afflicted the wider Fitzroy family. Fitzroy's uncle had already cut his own throat during a temporary fit of madness (well, permanent I guess, since it killed him) and Fitz himself had the occasional fantasy about topping himself. In hindsight I probably should have let him.

But to Fitz's credit, he was sufficiently self-aware to admit that the heavy responsibility of a long and dangerous sea voyage might not be ideal therapy for a manic-depressive, so he sought a companion to distract him.

Since it was unpaid, only rich kids qualified. Moreover the successful applicant would have to be equally comfortable with his own company as much as Fitz's, because Fitz knew he could be as grumpy as a grizzly when the affliction took him.

This pretty-well narrowed it down to Charles Darwin, who had the knack of getting on with everyone, including himself. So Charlie went a-cruising on the Beagle, and all was nearly lost. This extraordinary confluence of unlikely events is perfectly captured in this paraphrased early poem:

For want of a nail the shoe was lost,
For want of a shoe the horse was lost,
For want of a horse the rider was lost.
For want of a Prozac, Fitzroy invited Darwin onto the
Beagle.

The theory of evolution therefore, is as much a product of Fitzroy's madness as it is of Darwin's insights; yet no one gets taught that at school, do they?

Mind you, Charlie was no model of health either. Since I'd had no success changing his line of interest, I worked long and hard at limiting how much time he could spend working on it, by hitting him again and again with everything at my substantial disposal, including malaise, vertigo, dizziness, muscle spasms, tremors, vomiting, cramps, colic, bloating, incessant farting, headaches, blurry vision, severe tiredness, nervous exhaustion, dyspepsia, blisters, eczema, weeping, anxiety, panic attack, fainting, heart palpitations, insomnia, tinnitus, and my old favourite, depression. He was a walking Medicare nightmare, but he was nothing if not determined.

No matter what I threw at him, it became clear to me that he wasn't going to quit his infernal pursuits. Even the Great Random threw a few obstacles in his path, like earthquakes in New Zealand and storms in the Atlantic and volcanoes in the Galapagos and terror in Tierra del Fuego. But nothing would divert the infernal man from penning his pitiless tome that needed a half a bloody page just for the title:

On the origin of Species
by Natural Selection
or
The Preservation of Favoured Races
in the Struggle for Life.

In it Charlie questioned everything about life that had hitherto been attributed to me. Plants and animals of every kind were explained in one fell swoop. Everything that is, except humans.

There was only one line in the entire book about humans; a single line among thousands, which made a casual suggestion that humans might be descendent from animals. Well, it was like the whole of England read only that line and ignored the rest of the book. That single line annoyed the entire nation of Great Britain and a fair chunk of Europe and America too, because it seemed to imply that humans and apes had a common ancestor.

Well duh! I knew that was correct of course since I was born inside the head of one of them – my dear old mommy Muktuk – and I'd watched the entire process evolve through to the present day. I thought it would have been obvious to even the dullest of observers that it was true, so I was quite surprised to find that most people were insulted by the suggestion.

People absolutely hated the idea they might be descendent from hairy creatures that sniffed their own backsides; although decency demanded they find a more elegant argument, so they chose appearance. They couldn't possibly be related to apes because they looked so different from them.

Charlie got attacked from all sides; religion, politics, women, family, friends and even strangers. They all demanded proof of a missing link that could provide the tiniest shred of supporting evidence for the transition from monkeys to men. Unfortunately for Charlie he couldn't show them any fossils to demonstrate what he was thinking, because none had been discovered yet. But in reality he didn't need to.

At the time I was a bit surprised he didn't just point to a mother and her son and say they looked and acted very differently to each other, but there was no missing link between *them*, so what was their point? Difference didn't need a missing link. Dog breeders had known it for centuries so I was quite surprised they didn't speak up in Charlie's defence.

The differences between even two Londoners, let alone say, a three-week-old Nigerian baby girl and a fifty-year-old Icelandic fisherman were surely enough to demonstrate that evolution was taking place before their very eyes. Yet people seemed to be in complete denial that they were as different looking from each other as they were from apes, and I now believe that Madam Self Delusion had been working overtime inside their heads.

She must have convinced them they were all identical clones or something; that they'd never looked in a mirror nor seen the obvious differences between themselves and anyone standing next to them. Either that, or people were significantly denser that I'd realized, which is another possibility, I suppose.

As for whether Charlie's theory was right about humans having evolved from green slime, I can't say. I wasn't around then and neither was anyone else, but it's the most plausible hypothesis I'd heard thus far, notwithstanding the insult to green slime. But no, most people clung to any piece of driftwood they could grasp to keep themselves afloat in their particular river of trust; and the favourite one was that I had created them as a one-off special. Apes had nothing to do with it.

Everyone from Sharmah to Luther insisted that I had created all things bright and beautiful. And I've certainly done nothing to change that weird opinion (why should I?). But clearly the vast majority of plants and animals existed well before god-me popped up to supposedly create them.

Madam Self Delusion knows this, because she's been around a lot longer than I have. When she was just a wee lass tinkering with primeval self-esteem, the world was already full of organised molecules that you'd call life. And I mean really well organised molecules – like trees and fish and insects and birds and dinosaurs and mushrooms and *Yersinia pestis* and so on. They'd already created themselves without any help from me. Yet the people of Charlie's day really hated (many still hate) the idea that things could create themselves given enough time. They preferred the delusion that a Being had to do the creating. That way they could feel good about their own abilities to create things. People really are awfully precious sometimes, and worry about the pettiest things.

Nevertheless, despite the massive counter insurgency by most of England, Charlie's theory found a tentative foothold in academia, like one of his darling mussels clinging to a wave-swept rock, and soon began to grow into accepted truth. It looked like the game was up for me. For the first time since Muktuk I understood what humans meant when they said they felt threatened. I don't mind admitting I was down in the imaginary mouth for a while, and I started writing my own eulogy. I was sure I was going to die one day. How's that for self-belief?

Then it hit me like shot of bad tequila that I'd been approaching this supposed problem the wrong way. I'd forgotten my roots. I'd grown so hubristic in my all-powerful Supreme Being format that I'd forgotten that my various Joey, God and Allah versions were just three of many ways I could exist inside people's minds. How could I have forgotten that? I had to go all the way back to Sharmah to remember how I boarded this religion train in the first place – a train I'd been on so long I'd forgotten there were other tracks.

Bloody Sharmah! He was the one who'd had the epileptic fit and pretended he'd been to the afterlife, and invented *spiritual* and all that stuff that made us both so giddy with power. It all stemmed from him and that tiny moment of insanity in his otherwise insignificant cyst-ridden head. Everything that humankind had become stemmed from that tiny point in pre-history and I had been sucked along with it, surfing its glorious but misguided power-wave as if it would never break. And in doing so I had inadvertently transferred Sharmah's insanity into every mind on the planet, programming your gullible minds with a virus that infected not living tissue, but common sense.

Was it really possible for an entire species to be insane? Could billions of people believe in things that didn't really exist, and still manage to survive, let alone thrive the way you lot have? It seemed so unlikely that I'd never seriously considered it before; yet now I look back objectively I can't fault the proposition.

I'm faced with overwhelming evidence that everyone on Earth has a learned mental virus of which I'm both donor and doctor; poacher and gamekeeper. What other explanation is there? Sane people wouldn't pretend false things were true just so they could kill other people that wouldn't pretend along with them, would they?

I'm really asking you: 'WOULD THEY?'

If I were forced to think up a definition of insanity, the following would surely pass muster as a first attempt: *Pretend something exists when it clearly doesn't, then kill everyone who won't play along*.

Yet this is exactly what had been happening for the past ten thousand years. How come nobody noticed? People normally got locked up for doing a lot less than that, but in my entire journey from Muktuk to Darwin I don't remember a single murder or torture in my name, or genocide for that matter, that the perpetrators ever attributed to their own insanity. And I should know; I've been inside every mind that ever executed such horrific deeds. I'm prepared to swear under oath that each man supervising the butchery considered himself to be perfectly sane, and that his actions were entirely justified on the basis of preserving his self-esteem. His victims believed the wrong things – they had to be eliminated, or he would have been forced to look inside himself, threatening his own self-esteem.

I am still in an excellent position to make this judgment by the way, because I have been, and still am inside quite a few certified insane people. Not all, of course because some of them can't grasp they are going to die one day; but of the ones I have been inside of, they all knew they were insane. This is an oddity of mental illness I won't delve into here other than to say that deep down most mentally ill people know they aren't quite right in the head, and can recognize that their behaviour is odd, even if they can't do anything about it.

But the folks I'm talking about – the ones that kill and torture on my behalf – have no earthly idea that they are nuts. They're convinced they're perfectly sane. Indeed nowadays I would be hard pressed to find enough sane people for a side-by-side comparison. And therein lies the rub: without realizing it until Darwin gave me an intimate understanding of natural selection, it turns out I'd been artificially selecting for people predisposed to insanity – sadly at the expense of the sane ones.

Over the years my dominant nutters have killed off almost all the rational people – or at least frightened them into feigning insanity – which surely explains why there are so few mentally balanced people left on Earth to compare them with.

Without knowing it, I'd been doing precisely what Samuel Taylor Coleridge said could not be done – I'd been Darwinizing with a Vengeance – creating not lions out of leopards as he'd speculated mockingly, but instead creating fools out of the faithful. Moreover I've been doing it with such blind zeal and pitiless efficiency that insanity has become the standard human condition.

Had I really turned the entire world into a loony bin? The notion was so abhorrent that for a while I favoured a different, though only slightly more palatable explanation: that Earth was already a galactic lunatic asylum well before I came along, to which the rest of the Universe sent their genetically deranged dross. Indeed I'd almost convinced myself of this until it occurred to me that if it were true there'd surely have to be unbreakable rules against breeding. People would surely be restricted to unproductive sex, and not be allowed to fill up the planet with babies the way they'd been doing.

Another problem with that explanation was this particular insanity isn't genetic. Kids aren't born with their parents' insanity hard-wired; they have to acquire it later in life. I never caught a kid killing an adult for not believing in Santa Clause; or torturing grandma for not worshiping the tooth fairy. No, this particular insanity comes later in life like Huntington's disease or Alzheimer's. But instead of it waiting in ambush like Sharmah's mammoth hunters, the disease shows itself only when kids become susceptible to communication. Kiddies have to be taught how to believe crazy things and act crazy, as soon as they can understand the language of their parents. In this way the disease can sit and incubate during puberty and present in its most infectious form during adulthood, to be then passed on to the next generation. It`s all about nurture; nature has nothing to do with it.

So now I'm forced to admit to you (and to myself, damn it) that my inadvertent creation of religion is the only non cellular form of contagious insanity that exists – not counting rap music.

Sorry about that.

14

WORLD DOMINATION

After Darwin's revelation, I was tempted to fess-up to everybody that all this afterlife stuff they'd been taking so seriously was really just make-believe; that it was actually made up by a smelly little Stone Age slacker called Sharmah, who made it up in the hope of getting more food and sex, and whose only inspiration was an effective but short-lived technique for killing mammoths. How's that for a religious foundation? I thought it might have been fun to watch all seven billion of you stop in your tracks and slap your foreheads in unison. The resounding 'doh!' would probably have shattered mountains, or at the very least started a sizable hurricane.

But then it occurred to me that probably nothing would change. I'm continually gob-smacked at humanity's addiction to Madam Self Delusion's charms, and the things they'll pretend are true just so they can hang on to a tiny speck of misguided self-esteem. I'm also amazed at how rarely I have to suggest horrible things for people to do to each other to defend their self delusion. Humans apparently have an in-built catalogue of nasties to draw from without any internal prompting from me. It's as if the human brain is predisposed to making up nonsense for the sole purpose of slapping people around who won't agree with it. People's brains are so addicted, that if I told them I've been conning them all these years they probably wouldn't believe me. The river of trust is just too wide now and they can't see the bank.

I can't believe I'm admitting this, but perhaps I'm partly to blame. I don't deny that when I realized humans were so gullible I took unfair advantage. I encouraged my own proliferation by tapping into the very worst of what humans were and are capable – appealing to lust, greed and primal fear just so I could climb the hierarchy of brain controllers. And I don't deny it was fun recruiting Madam Self Delusion to see what tricks she could turn to my advantage.

But I must admit the game got a tad out of control, and now one third of the human race hates another third, while the remaining third hates them both, and they all pray to me daily to kill everyone they don't like. I mean, SHEESH! Can't you all just grow up and laugh it off? The Earth and everything on it is doomed to burn anyway. Why make the ride any worse than it has to be?

During these moments of weakness I can't help wondering what a nourishing and bountiful place Earth might have become if I'd just stuck to the basics; occasionally reminding people that they are going to die one day then letting them go back to picking berries. If I hadn't made self delusion so fashionable would there be more people on earth now, or fewer? Would it be a happier place, or more violent? These are questions that used to occupy me a lot once, but since I'm the only one that's ever going to care about the answers, they really don't matter so much anymore. I'll still occupy every mind in the world; and whether they'll call me Joey or God or Allah, or even Destiny, all minds will still belong to me.

In many ways I'm glad Darwin broke the myth about me. He might even prove to be the antidote for this virus that I've been unwittingly spreading throughout the human collective. If so, good on him; I really don't mind. My original pure strain, namely *you are going to die one day*, will still continue to corner the market; and that's really all that matters.

Speaking of markets, I think it's interesting to estimate how big my market might get. As you've seen I'm not good at predictions but I'm fairly certain that people will keep on multiplying *ad nauseam* until something other than good sense shuts them down. Assuming the upper limit of propagation is a place to stand on dry land, then if everybody stands side by side, front to back army-style, by my calculations the Earth's hundred and fifty trillion square meters of dry land should be able to hold about six hundred trillion people, albeit for just a few minutes till someone falls over.

But if they built one enormous building on all that dry land, rising up to the altitude at which breathable atmosphere stops – about eight thousand metres if dead Everest climbers are anything to go by – and they fitted that building with four thousand floors each two metres high so no one had to stoop, then we could multiply that six hundred trillion people by about thirty-five hundred. That's two quintillion people give or take a trillion, which for the visually minded among you is a two with eighteen zeros after it.

But that's not the theoretical limit either. Why not extend the building over the oceans until the entire planet is a four thousand storey building? In that case the maximum population would quadruple to eight quintillion.

But wait, there's more. A building has to be made of something. To build it, someone would need a lot of concrete and bricks and other materials drawn from the Earth's crust, which would leave a cave underneath the dry-land part of our building deep enough to house another six hundred trillion people, making a grand total of eight quintillion, six hundred trillion, which is really quite a market in anyone's math.

Moreover, it should be sobering for people to realise they will only stay alive if they keep their heads within the confines of this wispy cloud of unique gas mixture they call atmosphere. It's twelve-thousand kilometres wide and eight kilometres thin. They, like you, are trapped in it like bacteria confined to the swirly film of a soap bubble – which amazingly is about the same ratio of diameter to thinness.

Poke your head above or below the bubble's film and you're dead. Cloud it with poison and you're dead. Make it radioactive and you're dead. That's right: dead, dead, dead, as I've been telling you all these millennia. Still, you're going to die anyway so I suppose it's up to you how you achieve it.

As far as I can tell there aren't any other bubbles of life-sustaining atmosphere anywhere else in the Universe, so I would have expected people to really take care of this one. Well... sane people would, but you already know my thoughts on that subject. As I said, it should be sobering; but it doesn't seem to be.

So there we have the upper limit of what's potentially available to me. I can't imagine an alien race will be visiting anytime soon, in which I might find new and more interesting minds to tinker with. I think now you can understand why I get despondent from time to time, and why I've resorted to forcing this unfortunate typist to unwittingly type and publish my story, and hopefully broadcast it into space. Don't judge him too harshly by the way – he had no choice in the matter. I control him exactly the same way I control you.

But if aliens do arrive unexpectedly, I promise I'll be more careful. If they can understand they are going to die one day, I won't put them on the religion train like I did with you guys. I understand now that the train just goes round and round, round and round, round and round, leading absolutely nowhere, except to pump up the self-esteem and erections of a few inadequate men, which hardly justifies the effort. And if you still don't want to believe it's all about male sexual obsession, just ask yourself this: *How come there aren't any religions run by women?*

Come on...think about it! Don't just read on without thinking!

How come there aren't any religions run by women?

Yes, that's right. Because religious leaders all start off having unresolved sex issues; and power at your expense is the only way they can think of for dealing with it.

Now do you get it? Yes? At last?

At last.

So, from now on I'll be staying away from religious deception, and will instead stick to my most basic form: that everybody dies one day. In this form I'll live forever; literally too big to fail, since by definition I can't die until the last of you dies.

I used to fantasize that someone might come along and mutate me into a catalyst – an intellectual enzyme perhaps – so I could stimulate the creation of a new, more intelligent, more socially responsible species than your current *Homo Sapiens,* which laughingly means Wise Man. If that happens I'll try to create a species driven by mutual interest rather than mutual fear – a kind of human beehive if you like – in a land of honey at least, if not milk, in which everyone gets exactly the same pleasure hit from common interest as they currently get from self interest. Nothing would be lost. You would all still strive to feel smug about winning. Your self-esteem would remain intact. You'd simply be striving to cooperate rather than show off. Chemicals would still make you decide what was worth striving for and what wasn't. You'd still be fleshy puppets to your hormonal strings as you are now. You wouldn't know any different; you'd just be a whole lot happier. But every time someone comes along with such a brilliant suggestion, one of my well-trained zealots kills her, making us all tragic victims of my fabulous success.

So, from now on I'll be sticking to my most basic form: that everybody dies one day. Like I said, I'm essentially immortal; literally too big to fail since I can't die until the last of you dies, which is still a long way off. Nothing much will change for me between now and then, until the sun blows up. It's surely too late for your current species to change – a species that could be more accurately named *Homo Myopicus,* or Short-Sighted Man. Never mind; intelligent life might pop up somewhere eventually.

In fairness your low IQ's aren't entirely your fault. Wisdom can never be your hallmark despite the name you gave your species; you're just not wired up that way. Having spent a million years inside your brain, I've acquired a pretty good understanding of its design; and the bad news is it's a very poor learner.

What's clear to me is that over the eons your brain has organised itself with just one thing in mind: surviving just long enough to make a new one. Acquiring knowledge along the way has been a secondary consideration, and only judged to be worth the effort if it aided in the aforementioned single-minded pursuit of survival. Even then the effort could only be judged in hindsight, because if you didn't survive you didn't get to judge.

Back in your prehistory, it was never the smartest thinkers that went on to make more of themselves; it was the best survivors. And you've simply inherited whatever helped them survive, even though that inheritance may be quite useless in today's world. Sometimes being smart meant surviving, sometimes it didn't; which incidentally explains why Sharmah left no descendents. His family tree got chopped down as he choked to death on medium-rare mammoth filet while spinning one of his nonsense yarns to someone else's kids instead of his own.

Sharmah was smart but he never used his smarts to convince a female to make a baby with his sperm. Nor did he use what meagre wisdom he'd accumulated in his twenty-two years to recognize that bragging with a mouth full of food was an unnecessary risk to take, especially in a world already chock-full of necessary ones. Thus his potentially valuable genes never made it into a next version. But even if they had, there was still no way to predict if his issue would have done any better. Survival value can only be declared after survival has occurred. How smart your parents were counts for little.

As I mentioned earlier, each generation is born empty-headed, and must therefore start from scratch; to learn how to survive all over again, and find a mate, or not, as the case may be. The accumulation of knowledge in the hope it might prove useful beyond your own short lifetime has never been a criterion in brain design. Knowledge might be power, but it isn't wisdom. Your brain is a survivor not a sage, and is unlikely to act wisely except by chance. It's not your fault; it's simply a design flaw that evolution has yet to remedy. Personally I wouldn't worry about it.

So given that we're both stuck with our imperfections for the foreseeable future, I make this final plea: When the inevitable day arrives and the Sun bloats beyond Mars; the inferno engulfing the Earth will of course incinerate books as well as readers. Before it gets too hot, and if anyone feels so inclined before it's too late, I would very much appreciate if they would broadcast these words to the far reaches of the Universe in the hope that anyone listening might learn the lesson (which I had to destroy an entire species to learn) that world domination isn't really all it's cracked up to be.

Goodbye and good luck,

Joey God-Allah

16 March 2009
P.S. You're going to die one day.

ABOUT THE AUTHOR

Frank Aquino is an Australian-born author living in Perth. He is a successful petroleum engineer and now chooses to write for a living. His first book The Fremantle Doctor was published by New Holland Publishing in Sydney, and he has written a further seven novels so far. His stories, mostly adventure thrillers, are exciting and credible and cover a wide range of subjects relevant to today's troubled world, including politics, terrorism, religion and euthanasia. He loves kids, dogs, science, engineering and electronics. He also likes mechanical improvisation, which is evident in alter ego Ed Bailey, the protagonist in the Australian Coup series of books. When Frank's not writing he's tinkering in his workshop, or walking Toby the dog. Frank publishes in Australia through Blencowe Books